CHANGING MICHAEL

Jeff Schilling

bancroft
press

Cover Design: Steve Parke
Interior Design: Tracy Copes

Published by Bancroft Press
"Books that Enlighten"
410-358-0658
P.O. Box 65360, Baltimore, MD 21209
410-764-1967 (fax)
www.bancroftpress.com

ISBN 978-1-61088-122-7 (HC)
Printed in the United States of America

For my daughter, Maggie

CHAPTER 1

I never really thought much about Michael. He was like a stunted plant or a faded beige wall. I knew someone named Michael existed, but I didn't *know* him.

And he wasn't *that* weird.

There are degrees of weirdness, and weird can be good or bad or somewhere in-between. Bad weird is doing mean things to your pets. Good weird is answering the door nude when religious nuts drop by to save your soul. Convincing yourself that you're really Wonder Woman is somewhere in-between, but closer to bad than good.

Being gay isn't weird. Pretending to be straight when you think you're gay is a little odd, but not as weird as wearing tinfoil on your head so the government can't read your thoughts.

I think I'm gay, but I'm not stupid, so I pretend I'm straight. I may be weird but not stupid. Pretending gives me an advantage. The less *anyone* knows about you, the better.

Everybody's weird. Some people just have a higher percentage of weirdness.

Anyway, on the outside, Michael wasn't that weird. High school senior, sort of tall, but the gangly, awkward kind of tall. Hair that was a bit too long in front and a little too short in back; hair that was parted in exactly the wrong spot and always looked like he'd taken a stab at cutting it himself.

Michael was smart, but in a way that made people often uncomfortable rather than envious. He was the kind of kid who would often come up with the answer before anyone else, or ask a question that would baffle kids and educators alike. The kind of question that gets a, "Well, I'm afraid we're running short on time, so we need to move on."

Michael walked with his head thrust forward, kind of like a bull with its eyes glued to the floor. It was like he'd fallen through a trap door recently and wasn't about to let it happen twice. He didn't run through the halls, but his stride was a little too choppy to qualify as walking. And when he was in a hurry, the hair in front would start to flop.

In short, Michael seemed to enjoy making his time at school far more unpleasant than necessary. As a result, most of us just assumed Michael had the *bad* kind of weirdness inside as well as outside. And the combination relegated Michael to a fairly low caste in the high school system—one that had to endure mental and, sometimes, physical abuse on a regular basis at Alexander High School.

To be honest, though, the Michael abuse wasn't something that really caught my attention. Like I said, he barely registered. But the day I got sucked in was different. Looking back, I blame my mom. No particular reason, other than I enjoy pinning the blame on Mom. It always gets her going, which is usually pretty amusing.

But at this point, the whole thing has gotten out of hand and someone needs to be held responsible.

And I'm not about to take the blame.

"What's wrong?" Mom asked.

I shrugged.

We were sitting at the kitchen table in-between stacks of Mom's work papers. She's some kind of accountant, I believe. Or auditor. She could be a coroner, though; she definitely has the demeanor.

Anyway, even though Mom does, in fact, have a designated "office" that includes four walls and an actual desk, she prefers the kitchen table.

It was early—I usually don't roll out of bed until I hear, ". . . and this is the *last* time I'm going to come in here." I have an alarm clock but prefer Mom. In order to use the snooze feature on my clock, you actually have to reach up and touch the right button. With the Mom Method, I eliminate the need to physically move until I absolutely have to. This might sound a bit extreme, but it can sometimes mean an extra twenty minutes of sleep.

It also succeeds in getting Mom nice and wound up before I even get out of bed.

Anyway, it was early and I was sitting at the breakfast table, a slice of unappealing toast parked in front of me. It was just me and Mom; Dad's never around in the morning.

I sighed.

"What's wrong, Matthew?" she said again, this time in her put-upon tone of voice.

I watched her from the corner of my eye as she scanned the piles of paper, looking for something.

I gave a second, smaller shrug.

"Don't tell me then," she said, taking a sip of coffee.

Although I wasn't hungry, I was a bit irked that Mom thought she could get away with offering her only child a slice of burnt toast with an uneven scrape of butter.

Mom glanced sideways at me, then over at the microwave clock.

"We need to get moving," she said.

I absently poked at my toast, putting a hole in it.

"You *will* be eating that before we leave," she said.

"No," I said, sadly. "I'm afraid someone put a hole in it."

"You're still going to eat it. I don't care what you did to it."

"Me?"

"Matthew, I watched you do it."

"Untrue. I would never desecrate a good piece of toast. Besides, you were looking at your papers."

No response.

Apparently, Mom was preoccupied. Interacting with someone who's preoccupied irritates me. If she couldn't prepare a better breakfast, the least she could do was give me her undivided attention. It's hard to believe she doesn't know that by now.

"Did you hear me use the word 'desecrate'?" I asked.

"I did. Marvelous," she muttered. She leaned over the table, squinting at a pile of documents on the opposite side.

I shook my head.

She glanced at the clock again and said, "Okay, why don't you—"

"Can I have some juice?" I asked, politely.

Mom turned to look at me.

"You see I'm busy, right?"

I brought a hand to my throat. "It's just . . . I feel like I might be getting a sore throat," I whispered, "and I really don't want to miss school today."

Mom stared. I swallowed, grimacing painfully.

She narrowed her eyes and started to open her mouth, but closed it and sighed.

"Are you okay?" I rasped. "Are you sick, too?"

I watched her jaw muscles clench.

"You need to drink this quickly," she soon said as she returned from the refrigerator. "We're leaving in five minutes."

I accepted the glass, mouthing the words "thank you."

Mom crossed her arms. I took a delicate sip and winced. She rolled her eyes but didn't say anything. I watched as her eyes were drawn back toward her piles.

"Big project?" I wheezed.

"Yep."

One of the stacks seemingly called to her. She moved toward it, hand extended.

"Need any help?"

"Help?"

I nodded at the stacks.

"No, thank you. I just need you to hurry up."

I set my glass down thoughtfully, then pulled a few papers from the nearest stack.

"Here you go," I said, handing them to her.

"Matthew! No—I have everything organized. Where did you get those?"

The papers were whisked from my hand. Glaring down at the table, she tried to find the correct pile.

"Sorry," I said, hoarsely. "Just trying to help."

"As I said, you can help me by—"

"You know I'm always happy to help."

Mom snorted.

"What?" I asked, looking surprised. "I'm a *very* helpful person."

Mom laughed. It was the short, annoying variety.

"You don't think I'm helpful?" I asked.

"Finish the juice and get your backpack," she snapped.

"You're hurtful," I said, picking up my glass.

"Uh-huh."

"I'm just trying to help."

"Matthew! Get ready!"

"What about my toast?" I asked.

"What about it?"

"I'm hungry," I said.

"Then take it in the car."

"But someone put a hole in it."

Her hands were now on her hips. I gave myself a point.

"Get ready for school . . . *now.*"

"Of course," I said, standing. "Whatever I can do to make things a little easier."

"Let me tell you something, young man. This is the *last* time I—"

A car horn blared. I gave myself an additional point.

"What was that?" Mom said, turning toward the front of the house.

"Jack," I said, polishing off the juice and wiping my mouth. "Got to go."

I almost made it out of the kitchen.

"Just a minute!"

I turned, eyes wide. "Yes?"

"Jack's here?" she said.

"Yep," I said, turning to go.

Jack's a friend from school. Well, not a "friend" exactly. I don't have many of those. Friendships require a bit too much give and take. I prefer taking. I guess Jack's what I would call a "close acquaintance." It's somewhere above "classmate" but below "friend."

"You're riding with Jack?" Mom asked, slowly.

"Yep."

Mom closed her eyes. I gave myself half a point.

"You've been closing your eyes a lot this morning," I said. "Did you get enough sleep last night?"

"When did you know you were riding with Jack?" she asked, struggling to control her volume.

"Last night." I said.

"Last night?"

"You're repeating yourself a lot, Mom. Sure you're okay?"

A hand came up to her eyes.

"Matthew?"

"Yes?"

"Just go."

"Love you, too!" I called, hurrying to the front door. I grabbed my backpack and shoved my toes halfway into my shoes.

She yelled something on my way out, but I accidentally pulled the door closed before she finished. I hurried down the front steps and toward Jack's car. Music leaked from the closed windows of his immaculate Oldsmobile Cutlass GR (Geriatric Ride).

Jack's car is two shades of blue. Light blue body with a dark blue roof made of some kind of squishy material. I believe it's the same stuff that covers the seats and most of the interior. Jack inherited his grandmother's car when she died and honors her memory by keeping it spotless, old lady-style.

"What's up?" Jack said as I slid in beside him.

"In a second," I said, glancing at the front door. "Better go."

I didn't have to say it twice. The engine whined and we shot backwards, plunging blindly into the street.

"Playing with Mom?" he said.

I nodded, pulling a shoe over my heel.

"How many points?" he asked.

"Two and a half."

"Nice," he said. Jack threw it into drive and the car lurched forward.

"Actually, three and a half: A 'Hands on Hips,' a 'Young Man,' a 'Last Time,' and at least one 'Eye Close,'" I said.

"Sweet."

As I mentioned, Jack's an acquaintance, but he's privy to more than most. For example, he knew the gist of the Mom Game, also known as Don't Tip the Parent. If you push too hard, there may be consequences. (Like loss of car privileges or loss of a digit—depends on the parent. My point: Know your target well.)

Considering the time limits, scoring three and a half points was a pretty good round. Of course, knowing I didn't have to ride to school with

Mom allowed me to take a few more risks.

All things considered, it was a strong start to the morning. I could feel a good day in the works.

And it was, for a while—that is, until I ran into Michael.

Jack and I skidded into the student parking lot—Jack's a bit stingy when it comes to using his brakes. After frightening the hell out of several students who heard the squealing tires and spotted Jack's Oldsmobile barreling toward them, he found the spot he was looking for.

"Little close, don't you think?" I asked.

We were at the end of the row, about as far from the school entrance as physically possible.

Jack didn't answer. He lifted himself a few inches from the driver's seat in an effort to get a better view of the yellow lines.

"Damn it," he said, quietly.

Jack shifted into reverse, backing the car into position for another try.

"There," he said, happily.

Jack had successfully managed to slide over the exact middle of a yellow line. Most assholes who feel they need two spaces do so to protect their priceless metal children. But I knew how Jack felt about his car.

"Why?" I asked.

"I don't know," he said, laughing. "Just feel like being a dick today."

"How is that different from any other day?"

We walked through the student parking lot toward Alexander Hamilton High School, pushing through the side entrance and past the cafeteria.

"You going to your locker?" Jack asked.

I shook my head. My locker was in the other direction. Considering Jack's comments in the parking lot, I was sure he'd get into some kind of altercation prior to first period, and I wanted to see it. I was genuinely surprised when we made it to my Astronomy classroom without an incident.

"Thanks for the ride," I said.

Jack nodded.

I watched him make his way down the far right of the hall, near the lockers. I watched him extend an arm, running his hand over the dangling locks, setting them in motion as he walked. Passing a small recess in the wall, Jack latched onto a bulky metal trashcan and pulled. It scared the shit out of almost everyone in the immediate vicinity when it came crashing to the floor.

I closed my eyes and shook my head, smiling.

Just one of the many reasons I enjoyed his company.

His *occasional* company.

CHAPTER 2

The bell rang, signaling the merciful conclusion of World History, a second period full of delightful surprises and riveting information. Nothing like a lecture full of dates and obscure treaties. And judging from our instructor's attire ("costume" is actually more accurate), as well as the unmerciful cosmetic-related beating she gave her face on a daily basis, I'm guessing her memories of high school aren't very Disney-like, because everything about her teaching style seems like an insidious, drawn-out form of revenge.

I collected my books and slowly headed for the door, in no hurry to get to English.

I had stopped in the hallway to scowl at a flyer for some upcoming play when I noticed Michael on the opposite side, pinned up against a locker.

I paused.

A little verbal harassment or a shove from behind wasn't terribly uncommon, but finding Michael up against a locker was somewhat unusual.

I pushed my way to the other side of the hall, wondering who had him.

Leonard.

Now it made sense. Leonard was definitely weird, and in his case there was no question what type. Leonard was the bad kind of weird, the kind of guy who would do something to the family cat.

I decided to see what I could do for Michael. No particular reason, other than an intense dislike of Leonard and a reluctance to go to English.

And, as I had *tried* to explain to my mom, I'm generally a helpful person.

"Hey, Leonard . . . Michael. What are you guys up to?"

You had to be careful how you handled Leonard. Actually exhibiting surprise or apprehension about his decision to slowly asphyxiate Michael might make him that much more interested in the process.

Leonard glanced at me without turning his head.

"Nothing."

Michael squirmed, but there wasn't much he could do. Leonard had a forearm across Michael's throat.

"Just hanging out?" I said.

"He was looking at me," Leonard said, increasing the pressure on Michael's throat.

Michael made little noises.

"You probably shouldn't strangle him, though."

"Why not?" he said with a smile.

"Willis is headed this way."

Mr. Willis is the principal.

"I don't give a shit about Willis," Leonard said, glaring at Michael as if he'd silently called for the principal's help.

"He looks pissed, though. Someone said he was looking for you."

"Why?" Leonard said.

"Chemistry lab's missing a few scales."

Leonard gave Michael's throat an angry shove and released him. "That was Dave," he said, turning to me. Michael held his throat and coughed.

"Then you'd better say something," I said, looking down the hall as if expecting Willis any minute.

"I'm not telling that asshole anything," he said, heading in the opposite direction. Leonard disappeared around the nearest corner. I turned my attention back to Michael.

"Lozenge?" I offered.

He shook his head, still coughing. Eventually, he decided he wasn't going to die and started walking.

"People don't like you much, huh?" I said, trailing after him.

He was headed toward the windows at the end of the hallway. He gave me an angry look and cleared his throat.

"Water?" I asked. "Hot tea? Maybe a little honey?"

"Why are you following me?" he asked, hoarsely.

We were coming to a set of stairs at the end of the hall. I slipped in front of Michael. My next class was on the second floor and I wasn't finished with him yet.

"I'm concerned, Michael," I said.

"What?"

"I'm a concerned peer."

He cleared his throat again.

"Would you like a poultice?"

Michael shook his head. Although I was in front of him, he somehow managed to fake me out and make it to the stairway. Rather than follow, I stepped over to the railing, watching him go.

"All right, then. We'll talk tomorrow!" I called.

Michael looked up. I smiled and waved.

He made a frowny face, then disappeared under my feet. The bell rang—a real delight, since it was very close and incredibly loud.

Time for English, I suppose.

I started to push away from the railing but saw Jack trudging up the stairs and waited.

"You're late for class," I said.

"Eat it," he replied. As we walked down the hall, he asked, "Who were you talking to?"

"Michael."

"Michael? Michael who?"

I told him.

"Why?" he asked, sourly.

"I'm not sure yet."

"Whatever," he said with a shrug.

We passed a group of girls acting loud and silly going the other way.

"Hi, Jack!" one called.

"Fudgepork!" Jack yelled back.

I looked back. The girls had stopped.

"What'd he say?" one asked.

"Fudge-something?"

"What's fudgepork, Jack?" I asked, stopping in front of my English classroom.

He smiled. "I don't know."

I watched him walk around a corner, wondering if he'd actually make it to his next class. Jack has some attendance issues.

The bell rang again, this time a little farther from my ear. I found my seat and fell into it. Ignoring Mrs. Brattleborough's request to take out something or other, I put a hand to my chin and stared absently at the front of the room. (I *think* her name's Mrs. Brattleborough, but I'm not entirely sure.)

Anyway, for some reason, I found myself thinking about Michael. Our little conversation in the hall had been brief and unsatisfactory. I'd pulled him out from under Leonard's smelly forearm and hadn't even received a "thank you."

The more I thought about it, the more it irritated me.

However, being the helpful, forgiving person I am, I decided to give Michael another opportunity to express his appreciation.

I decided I'd give him a day or so to realize the error of his ways and make amends. I'd even be open to accepting a small gift as a token of his remorse.

No sense holding a grudge, right?

CHAPTER 3

I found the perfect opportunity for Michael to make things right the next morning. Mom was working from home for the day, so I had the car, and I spotted him in the cafeteria on my way in from the parking lot.

It was early and the chairs were still upside-down, their legs in the air, their backs dangling over the edges of the tables. I noticed Michael huddled at the far end of the room, partially hidden behind the jungle of silver legs.

He heard me coming and glanced up, startled.

I grabbed a metal leg and flipped a chair down. I sat, facing him.

"Morning, Sunshine," I said.

No response. I studied him.

"You don't use conditioner, do you?" I said.

"What?"

"Your hair," I said, pointing.

"So?" he said, smoothing one side with the palm of his hand.

"It wouldn't look so bad if it wasn't plastered to your head."

He dropped his eyes.

"You do shampoo occasionally, right?"

"Yes," he snapped.

"Don't get testy with me."

"What do you want?"

I was about to force a little gratitude out of him when it occurred to me that Michael probably wasn't used to people actually working on his behalf.

So I explained it: "I'm here to help, Michael."

"What are you talking about?" Michael looked perplexed. He opened his book and tried to read, maybe hoping I'd go away. I snatched it from him instead.

"*Lud in the Mist*," I read. "Who's Lud?"

"Give me that, please," he said, as if it was a game he'd played too many times before.

"Not until you tell me who Lud is."

He sighed. "It's not a person; it's a place."

"Lud? How pretty," I said.

"Lud-in-the-Mist," he said. "It's a fictional English town."

"It's a ridiculous name."

Michael held out a hand.

I started to pass the book to him but pulled back when his fingers touched the cover. Then I thumped him lightly on the head.

We stared at each other again.

"Do you like the way things are?" I asked.

"What do you mean?"

"Do you like being the school weirdo?" I asked, handing the book back.

"Yes," he said, inspecting it for damage.

"Don't make me thump you again."

He sighed and looked up. "What people think about me isn't important."

"But wouldn't it be nice to walk to class without getting assaulted?"

He gave me a blank look.

I glanced at the parking lot out through the windows. Clumps of kids were drifting in from their cars.

"It doesn't matter," he muttered.

I stood up as voices began to spill down the hall and into the cafeteria.

"It does matter," I said.

"This world is transitory," he said, studying a blob of dried mustard at his feet.

"This world is *what*?"

Michael shook his head. Getting to his feet, he gently slid *Lud-in-the-Mist* into his backpack.

"Where are you going?" I asked as he slung his backpack over his shoulder.

"Class," he said.

"Want me to come?" I said, eager to miss the first few minutes of Astronomy.

He shook his head. Yet another helpful gesture slapped to the ground. It was becoming a pattern.

I watched him head for the door.

"See you soon!" I called.

He didn't turn.

I stood for a moment, considering. I'd now given Michael two opportunities to thank me and had come up empty-handed. There was simply no excuse for such behavior, especially when I had gone out of my way to perform an unsolicited good deed.

I decided we needed another conversation. And this time I was going to get something out of him, one way or another.

I ran into Jack on my way out of the cafeteria.

"What's up?" he said.

"Nothing. Just talking to my buddy Michael."

"Again?" he said.

"Yep."

"Why?" he said.

"Just curious."

We made our way down the hall, a small part of a growing stream.

"Hey, I talked to Jenny last night," Jack said, suddenly.

"Oh yeah?"

"Yep. That girl wants me."

One reason I avoid close friendships is the obligation to listen and respond to personal information that holds no interest whatsoever. One of the reasons I like Jack—he almost never shares. The only exception is "Girls Who Want Him." Apparently, the school is littered with them.

It wasn't hard to tune him out, though. If you're quiet and nod once in a while, people think you're listening. Or that you like them. Usually both.

We made our way around the knots and clusters of students. The halls aren't wide to begin with, so it doesn't take many people to go from almost empty to packed.

"Need to go to your locker?" Jack said.

I started to say "no" but changed my mind. My locker's on the second floor, and Jack's is on the first. I knew I'd see him at lunch, and I also knew I'd probably hear about Jenny again. I decided to pass on a double shot, since I wasn't interested in the first place.

"All right," Jack said. "See you at lunch."

"Yep."

Maybe I'd skip lunch.

"Hey, Matt," someone said once I was in Astronomy.

I held up a hand. "Got a test," I said.

"We don't have a test today."

"Different class."

I grabbed a dictionary from the bookshelf. "Transitory," I determined, means "temporary" or "fleeting."

Anyone who thought this world was "transitory" sounded like a jumper to me.

My interest in Michael grew just a bit.

Now I wanted both a "thank you" and some additional information on this "transitory" thing. I was fairly certain Michael wouldn't be very forthcoming, but perhaps he'd feel different outside of the school environment. *Should I make a house call?*

I took out a notebook and added a few features to the doodle I'd started earlier. (I'm an accomplished abstract doodler. I've toyed with the idea of letting the art teacher have a look, but she'd probably make a fuss and want to set up a showing and I'm not someone who needs that kind of validation.)

In any case, a house call seemed a bit much, but on the other hand, it was kind of intriguing.

Boredom is a constant problem for me, and the idea of forcing my way into Michael's house and making him uncomfortable held a certain appeal.

No, not *forcing. Finessing.*

I smiled.

Finessing my way in would be fun. Not only fun, but good practice. Michael had been challenging so far. Actually convincing him to let me in would be quite a coup.

Thinking about Michael's house and how I'd get past the front door almost kept me awake. However, five minutes of Mrs. Hammerschmidt's voice was enough to send me and half the class into a coma.

I tried to fight through it but lost.

Chapter 4

I should probably consider a career in law enforcement. I'm already a gifted detective. I wanted to catch Michael after school but wasn't sure which exit he'd take. I was pretty sure the student parking lot wasn't an option—if Michael had a car, it would have been well-known and occasionally vandalized. And as far as I knew, he didn't have (or ride with) any close friends.

Hence, my deduction: Michael either walked or took the bus.

Our school isn't too far from Washington, D.C. Maybe twenty minutes without traffic (something only absent between 3:30 a.m. and 3:45 a.m.). With traffic, it's anywhere from one to five hours. The greater Washington, D.C. area has been spreading outwards like an overflowing toilet for many years and will eventually flood all of Maryland and most of Virginia.

As a result, Alexander High School sits at the epicenter of suburbia, which means it's surrounded by housing developments.

These developments connect to other developments, and between each subdivision are strip malls, office buildings, and miles of traffic, on and on, forever and ever, amen.

But back to Michael.

I decided to conduct my stake-out in front of the school. I didn't think it would be too hard to spot him. I'd just look for the floppy hair.

Anyway, as I'm deep in thought, Michael pops out of the building and immediately scurries down the sidewalk past the waiting buses. He's already got a decent lead, so I take off running to catch up with him, but then realize I'm jogging by the parked buses and a captive audience, so I slow down to a fast walk instead—that is, until I remember how ridiculous speed walkers look. So, finally, I settle for a brisk but casual pace.

According to Mom (who is frequently unreliable), there was a small section of woods to one side of our school a long time ago. Now, a thick stand of townhouses has graciously replaced most of the unsightly trees. Once, I knew a few kids who lived in Village Oaks (although most of the oaks appeared to have been executed). On the other side of Alexander, the houses were older, smaller brick ones with a couple of unassuming apartment buildings thrown in for good measure. I knew the area but didn't know anyone on this side.

I followed Michael down the sidewalk and into the little brick neighborhood. I hung back a bit, not sure what he'd do if he realized I was following him. I figured his place had to be close. Even though the first few rows of houses seemed small, they were fairly tidy and not too bad.

But as we got farther away from the school, I knew the houses would get smaller and more dilapidated. Eventually, we hit a main road, and the houses at that end were pretty awful. It was like the builders, when they started working on the houses near the school, had been eager and energetic. But as they kept building, they got more and more tired and started to get a little sloppy, and by the end of the job, they just slapped everything together before lunch, left their trash and tools in the yard, and headed to the nearest bar for a three-day bender.

But I was pretty sure Michael didn't live down at that end.

Michael was a geek. Geeks live in nice, clean houses, with geeky parents who make lots of money programming computers to run the world.

Any minute now, I expected Michael to turn down a side road or into a front yard, but he just kept going, past the neater houses and past the bad ones, too.

And it wasn't just the houses. The yards we passed became more disheveled the farther we got from the school. Most were cluttered with rusting swing sets, or sprinkled with garbage instead of grass. Some had plastic toddler cars that looked as if either the sun or an older brother had set fire to part of the vehicle. One gutter that ran parallel to the sidewalk was an avid collector of crushed beer cans and filthy cigarette butts.

Back near the school, some of the houses had tight little garages that could accommodate one, maybe two clown cars on a good day. Down at this end, there was only the occasional carport, and the majority of these tilted in one direction or another and probably wouldn't make it past the next windy day.

I came around a slight bend in the road I was following; I could see the main road that intersected mine about a hundred yards ahead.

"What the heck?" I muttered, then wondered, *What if he doesn't live on this road? What if we've got another couple miles or something? What if it gets even worse?*

I was slowing a little, thinking perhaps I'd make a home visit some other time, when Michael *finally* turned down a driveway.

Not even a driveway really—just a section of broken asphalt. The chain-link fence around the front yard looked like someone had either dropped cinderblocks on it or driven a car into it a couple of times. Michael's house was a little brick box with small windows, brown grass, and pathetic little bushes near the front door.

A couple of broken-down cars had passed out across the weed-infested driveway. Their hoods were gone, and most of their engines were scattered beside them as if someone had torn through looking for an Easter egg.

Definitely not what I had expected.

It was the perfect house for Leonard, or someone who reeked of cigarettes and pot, but Michael was just a geek—the kind that reads science-fiction, plays *Magic*, and gets all flushed and out of breath describing a computer game. (I'd never actually seen Michael play *Magic* but figured it was a given.)

Michael had disappeared into the house when I got there. I stood near the fence, wondering if there was a mutant dog hiding around the corner, waiting for me to step into the yard. I opened the gate and swung it back and forth. The noise was loud enough to send any dog into hysterics. No barking.

Eventually, I stepped through and was halfway to the front door when someone popped out of a side door around the corner of the house. It was Michael, slouching down the driveway with a bag of trash. He stopped in his tracks when he saw me.

"What are you doing here?" he said.

"Selling knives."

It took him a moment to process the remark. I don't know whether he got it or not because he didn't bother to smile. Instead, he dropped the trash bag into a beat-up trashcan and took off down the sidewalk. I had a fence to deal with, so it took me a minute to catch up with him.

"No wonder no one comes to visit you," I said.

He turned on me like I'd slapped him.

"I came all this way just to see you. You're supposed to invite me in and feed me."

He relaxed a little, which meant he fell into his old slouch and walked off with his eyes glued to the street. We were on the sidewalk, moving away from his house and toward Route 30.

"Where we going?" I asked.

He glanced at me before answering. "Bookstore."

"Adult bookstore?"

"No."

"Why not?"

He didn't answer. I waited a moment, then said, "So this world is transitory, huh?"

Michael glanced at me. We were both on the sidewalk, although it was a pretty tight fit. We couldn't quite walk next to each other, so I was about half a pace behind.

Having a conversation with Michael was more than a little frustrating. Every time I made a comment, it was like offering food to a stray dog—Michael didn't seem to know whether I was going to hand him the food or give him a smack.

"Yes," he said.

"*Fleeting?*"

"Yes."

We came to the end of his street. Route 30 was clogged with traffic. Along this artery, strip malls and small office buildings elbowed each other for the best view. I was somewhat familiar with the area, but not enough to feel comfortable finding my way back to school if the bookstore was another half hour of side streets and shortcuts away.

Michael took a left, walking against the rushing traffic.

"Why's that?" I said.

"What do you mean?"

"Why is this world fleeting? It doesn't seem so fleeting to me," I said.

"So you're going to live forever?"

"Yes, Michael, I am."

We walked in silence for a while.

"You're not going to kill yourself, are you, Michael?" I asked.

Nothing.

"You're a troubled youth, aren't you?" I said.

"Why are you following me?"

"You're not a very good listener. I told you: 'I'm here to help.'"

Actually, I was there to see if I could convince Michael to let me in his house, but somehow we were getting farther and farther from it.

"I don't need help," said Michael, turning left and away from the noise of the road.

I stopped to watch.

"You can't run away from the people who care about you!" I yelled. "I know where you live!"

Michael stopped and stared.

"The bookstore's this way," he said.

"Oh."

"And could you please stop yelling?" he said as I caught up to him.

"Maybe."

The side street took us past a few more brick houses, although these were bigger than Michael's and more like the ones near school. Someone had converted one of the houses into a second-hand bookstore. The sign outside was hand-painted—a woman's face, with hair that grew and flowered like a vine: "Hole in the Wall Books."

"I'll bet she's magic," I said. "I wonder if she gets bees in her hair."

Michael ignored me. He bounded up the three stairs to the front stoop and barged through the door. Little bells rang as he disappeared inside.

I lingered at the bottom, watching the door as it shuddered to a close.

Do I really want to follow Michael into a used bookstore?

I hadn't been in many, but the handful I'd visited seemed to have a few things in common:

1) They smelled.

2) The people who worked inside were always very eager to help.

It would mean yet another sacrifice, and still more discomfort, but I'd come this far and felt I had to see things through.

I reluctantly turned the doorknob, sounded the little bells, and stepped in. As I imagined, the air inside was musty. Tall, mismatched bookcases formed a maze of tight passageways. No sign of Michael, but that didn't bother me. If I needed him, I'd just make a scene.

Here and there, little cardboard arrows pointed the way to "German Philosophers" and "Tolkien Lore." Not exactly "Fiction" versus "Nonfiction." I picked through a section devoted to elves and elf culture that eventually merged with dwarves and dwarf history. It was kind of cool, in a geeky sort of way.

I squatted down to look at the section on "Elf Culture."

I had to admit: Some of the covers were pretty interesting.

A city suspended in a giant tree. A dragon peering from behind a half-opened door in the middle of an overgrown field.

I started to feel like a little kid again. For a minute, I almost started to think like one—as if maybe, if I read these books, I'd know where to find the places on the covers.

Anyway, I could see why Michael was so into them. And I guessed it wouldn't take much to convince him that a bathroom door was actually a portal to an alternate universe.

And if my life was like Michael's, I'd probably take the first portal I found.

Speaking of Michael, where is he, anyway?

I stood up and almost had a heart attack.

Some dork in a stained green t-shirt was smiling at me from around a bookshelf. He had little round glasses and a chin beard that looked like a miniature mud flap.

"You like Eager?" Mud Flap asked.

It sounded like some kind of pick-up line.

"What?"

"You into Eager?" he repeated, nodding at the book in my hand.

"Oh," I said, noticing the name on the cover. "Not really."

"You should check it out," he said. "I think you'd like it."

"Yeah, thanks," I said, putting it back.

He kept smiling at me, so I opened my eyes real wide and stared. He got the message and pulled his fat head back around the bookcase.

I stood up, deciding I'd done enough research for one day. I headed down the aisle, took a few turns, and ended up right back with the elves and dwarves. I tried another direction, but then found myself in a corner surrounded by graphic novels, manga, and whatever else they call comic books.

There was a small, rectangular table in the middle of the alcove. Lidless white boxes were packed tight across every inch of surface space. In fact, the lucky boxes on the outside, stuffed with comics, actually hung over the edge of the table, a few inches too long. I decided to conduct a little physics experiment, wondering how many comics I could remove from the back of a box before it tipped forward and "accidentally" plummeted to the ground. It took some muscle, but I managed to wrestle a few free.

Each was encased in its own sterile sandwich bag. I paused, glancing at the covers. Apparently, I'd struck a set of *Silver Surfers*.

"Naked guy surfing," I muttered. I remembered my friend in the stained shirt. "Seems about right."

I tossed his erotic literature on top of the boxes, deciding to resume my search for the exit. This time, I found it.

I smacked the "someone's here" bells to see if anyone would come running, but no one did.

I was about to leave when I caught the edge of a conversation. I moved a little closer, down a narrow aisle that was almost a tunnel.

"Did your friend leave?" a voice asked.

"I don't know."

"Do you want to catch up with him?" the voice asked. "We can talk later."

"No."

I found a break in the shelves and peered through. I could just see Michael hunched over a wobbly stack of books on the floor. He reminded me of a caveman beside his kill. Mud Flap was standing above him, leaning against a bookshelf, arms folded.

"What's his name?" Flap asked.

"Who?"

"Your friend, Michael," he said patiently.

"He's not my friend. He just followed me here."

"Was he giving you a hard time?" Flap asked, straightening.

"No."

"Oh. I'm confused."

Michael sighed. "He helped me out the other day."

"Helped you?" asked Flap.

"This kid at school was bothering me."

Flap didn't say anything right away. Then, finally, he said, "Why?"

Michael looked up.

"You said he wasn't your friend, right?"

Michael nodded.

"So why did he get involved?"

"He said he wants to help me," Michael said.

"Help you *what?*"

Michael didn't answer. He pulled a book from the stack on the floor and studied the cover.

"Are you still having those dreams?"

Michael shrugged.

"Is that a yes?"

"Kind of."

"I'm concerned about the violence, Michael."

I raised my eyebrows.

"Have you called my doctor yet?" Flap asked.

"No."

"It's just someone to talk to, Michael. That's all it is."

"I talk to you, Jimmy."

Flap smiled. "But I'm just some guy who runs a bookstore. You need to get in touch with someone who knows what they're doing. Someone who can actually help you."

"You help me."

"Well, thanks, but . . ."

I decided to leave. The interesting part was over. Michael had violent dreams. Mud Flap's name was Jimmy.

Jimmy Flap.

Jimmy Flap corn and I don't care.

I made it to the front of the store, grabbed the bells with one hand, and opened the door with the other.

I said goodbye to the woman on the sign, the one with the flower hair, and walked back to the main road. It didn't take long to find Michael's street again.

On the way back to school to pick up my car, I realized that Michael was now more than a diversion. His violent dreams had lifted him to the status of passing interest. I decided to make a surprise visit to the cafeteria tomorrow before school. Jimmy Flap was right—he did need to talk to someone. There was something pathetic about the way he'd said, "But I talk to you, Jimmy." No one should have to talk to a guy with a mud flap.

I remember thinking the whole thing might actually turn into a good deed of some kind. It might even be possible to make a few tweaks and reduce the size of the target on Michael's back. Well, it would take more than a few tweaks, but you know what I mean.

I started to daydream, preparing for any interviews that might result from my noble work with Michael.

"So Matthew, tell me why someone like you, someone at the apex of the food chain, decided to help a bottom-feeder like Michael."

"Well, it was pretty clear to me that he desperately needed some help."

"And you say his only friend was some guy with a beard?"

"Mud flap, actually. Mud flap."

Falling asleep that night, I was almost looking forward to seeing Michael again. There was only one problem, though: The next day, Friday, Michael wasn't there.

CHAPTER 5

I had to find him.

Fortunately, Mom was working from home again. Getting the car on two consecutive days was unusual, so I had to deal with a few objections.

"What if I need to go to the store?" Mom complained.

"You're working from home," I said, taking the keys from their little hook over the writing desk in the kitchen.

"And?" she said, impatiently.

"And you should be working, not going on joyrides to the store."

In the middle of her response, I slipped into the garage, jumped in the car, strapped myself in, and waited. I sat for about thirty seconds, watching the door, then shrugged and pulled out of the garage.

I was glad to have the car but vaguely disappointed. I'd expected a better fight. It's not like the garage is half a mile from the kitchen. The least she could have done was scream at me from the door as I left.

It was a fairly quick trip by NOVA standards. On the way, I tried to work out an opening line—one that would at least get a foot in the door—but I found Michael's house too quickly.

It's important to have some lines ready when asking someone to do something they don't want to do. I always try to have a little something—even if it's not much.

I parked on the street and headed up the cracked asphalt to the side door. I still wasn't sure whether an angry dog lived behind the fence, and I wasn't about to get caught halfway to the front door when one rumbled around the corner of the house.

I banged on the thin metal door, trying to look through the cloudy plastic window. I couldn't see much—just the back of an ugly brown couch that looked like a piece of furniture you'd see at the end of someone's driveway with a sign that said "Free."

So here I am, squinting through the plastic, when this big fat stomach suddenly blocks my view.

Michael's father?

Beer gut, scraggly goatee, blue work shirt (untucked). Replace the blue shirt with a sleeveless white one and you'd have an exemplary ensemble.

"Yeah?" he said, pulling the door toward him.

I almost said, "You can't be Michael's dad. You're not a geek."

Instead, I said, "Michael home?"

"No. You know where he is?"

I paused for a minute. "Nooo . . . that's why I'm looking for him."

"Yeah, well, he left last night and didn't come back," Beer Gut said. "His mom's all upset."

"Why?"

"That's what *I* said," Gut said. "I keep tellin' her he'll come back when he gets hungry."

"You got that right."

"Probably at that bookstore," he said.

"Oh yeah?"

Gut nodded. "Playing that game or something. Probably ran up against a couple mean-ass dwarves and had to fight 'em all night."

I laughed. *Good one, Gut.*

"You want me to let you know if he's there?" I said.

Gut shook his head. "He's there. He don't have nowhere else to go."

"Want me to tell him you said 'hi'?"

"Tell him his mom's about to have a stroke," he said as he disappeared back inside.

Gut—you've get old if you had to live with him. And judging from our brief conversation, I figured it was a safe bet that Gut and Michael weren't best buds.

I could see Michael getting all worked up about something Gut said or did, which isn't productive at all. You need to study your opponents/ parents. Understanding the how and why of the parent is essential. You have to learn to distance yourself from your subjects. Otherwise, your work is tainted. If you let feelings get in the way, you'll never develop the techniques that will help you get what you want.

Obviously, Michael didn't know how to have fun with someone like Gut, an exercise that might make a good starting point for our "reconditioning."

Unfortunately, Michael was "sensitive." I was sure he took Gut seriously, and there's just no reason to take someone like Gut seriously. People like Gut remind me of dinosaurs—large creatures with walnut-sized brains. You'd think someone who reads all the time would be able to outsmart a dinosaur, but I guess not.

Anyway, I found my way to the bookstore again and parked near my girlfriend with the flowery hair. The sign could really use a swarm of angry bees fighting over her. Unfortunately, I'd need a Sharpie or paintbrush to do the job well, and I didn't have either. Besides, I'm really not much of a vandal.

I opened the front door two or three times and really got the bells going. I wanted everyone to know I was there. I didn't really feel like wandering around the little maze today.

Someone tapped my shoulder and I almost swung a fist. It was Jimmy Flap.

"I'm going to sue you if I have a heart attack in your store," I said.

"You won't get much," Flap said. He was smiling again. Now I knew he was trying to pick me up.

"I can tell. Is Michael here, or do you have him chained up in the basement somewhere?"

"Didn't I see you yesterday?" Flap asked, smiling.

I nodded.

"Maybe you could tell me your name," he said.

"Woodrow."

"As in Woodrow Wilson?" he asked.

"Exactly."

"Sorry, Woody—"

"Woodrow," I said.

"Michael stepped out, Woodrow. Anything I can help you with?"

"So he's been here?"

Flap didn't respond.

"Are you guys in the middle of some big *Magic* tournament?"

"No, that's in August," he said.

I checked his face, but it wasn't a joke.

"So does he sleep in an empty bookcase or something?"

"There's a futon in the back room," he said.

"I bet there is," I muttered.

"What's that?"

"Nothing."

"Sounds like you're pretty concerned about him," Jimmy Flap said, moving into a row of books.

"Very," I said, following.

"That's funny—Michael's never really mentioned you before," he said, rearranging a pile of thick reference books that had fallen across the floor.

"Oh, we go way back," I said.

"Which makes me wonder why he's never mentioned you."

"I'm pretty sure he mentioned me yesterday," I said, casually leaning against a shelf.

Flap looked up from the floor, but I just inspected my fingernails.

"That's interesting," he said, returning to the books. "I thought you'd left."

"I'm everywhere," I said.

"Really?"

I nodded. "I'm all-knowing."

"So you know about his mother?" Flap asked.

"Yep."

"You know about the car accident?"

"Yeah," I said, trying to frown.

"Then you know which arm she lost."

"The right one," I said. Fifty-fifty chance.

"She wasn't in a car accident," Flap said, taking a couple of books from the pile and heading down the row.

It took me a few seconds to recover.

"I know about his violent dreams," I tried, following.

"Do you?" he said, studying a shelf.

"Yep."

"What was the last one about?" he asked, finding a spot for one of the books.

"Violence?"

He smiled and continued around the corner.

"So when he goes Columbine, I'll just tell the police to come see you about the dreams," I said.

I turned the corner. Flap was standing in the aisle, studying the ground and stroking his beard.

"Do you have a special comb for that?" I asked.

He ignored me.

"You could mousse it into a point and carry a pitchfork. Girls like that kind of thing—guys, too."

Still stroking his beard, Flap set the remaining books on the floor and wandered toward the back of the store. I followed, ready to repeat my last thought in case he hadn't heard. We took a couple of sharp turns and ended up by a half-door a little higher than my waist. Behind it was a small, crowded room about the size of an extra-wide closet.

There was a desk pushed against one wall. The surface was nearly covered with scraps of paper, disorderly files and of course, more books. In the center of the mess was a little adding machine as well as a phone.

On the floor and braced against the walls were stacks of books. Their heights varied. It reminded me of one of those aerial shots of the high-rises crowded around Central Park.

Facing the desk was a battered and faded leather office chair that Flap had obviously rescued from the dump. The seat had seen a lot of oversized asses in its time and looked ready to give out.

Flap opened the half-door and closed himself inside.

"Don't I get to come in?" I asked.

Flap didn't answer. He took out his wallet and sat down.

"You don't have to pay me for my time," I said.

Flap found what he wanted: a little white business card.

"Who're you calling?"

"Hi, Suzi? It's Jim Murphy," Flap began. "Is Dr. Evans available? Can you have him call me as soon as he's free? Well, it's not an emergency, but I need to speak with him today . . . No, I'm okay. It's about a friend of mine. Something we've discussed before. Can you tell him it's about Michael? He'll understand."

What is he doing?

"Yep, I'll be around then. Great. Great. Thanks, Suzi. Oh, sure. It's 9-7-5 . . ."

Flap finished giving out his phone number, but I don't really hate Flap, so I'm not going to repeat it.

"Thanks again. Okay. You too. Bye."

"Who did you call?" I said.

Flap leaned forward in his chair and shoved his wallet into his back pocket. It looked like a tight squeeze.

"Are you going to buy anything?" Flap asked.

"No."

"Are you going to look for anything?"

"No."

"Then why are you here?"

"I like your company."

"Now I know you're lying," he said with a laugh.

"Yeah, that's a good one, all right," I said, imitating his laugh.

The "someone's here" bells suddenly came to life.

"I'll get it," I said.

"Get back here," Flap said.

Too bad he was behind his special little half-door. I wove my way through the aisles and almost slammed into Michael.

"Careful," I said. "Your friend's calling people about you."

"Huh?" As usual, Michael looked completely baffled.

"Some doctor. Sounds like he's going to have you committed."

"That's enough," said Flap, pulling up beside us.

What with the excitement of escaping from the room behind the half-door and having to hurry to the front of his store, he was a little out of breath, so his "firm tone of voice" wasn't very effective.

"Oh, so you didn't call?" I said.

"You need to mind your own business," he snapped.

"What's going on?" Michael said.

"Michael, I need to talk to you . . . privately," Flap said.

"Careful, Michael," I said.

"Ignore him."

"I'll help you, Michael," I said.

"Michael, he's just—hey, hold on a second."

Michael headed for the door.

"Michael, wait up!" I called.

Flap tried to grab my shoulder, but I slipped by him, caught the closing door, and squeezed out.

"Michael!" Flap called from the door.

Michael didn't look back.

"Call me later, okay?" Flap tried.

I trotted up behind Michael and put a hand on his shoulder. He shrugged it off.

"Come on, man," I said. "Slow down."

"Why?" he asked, turning to face me. "So it doesn't look like you're chasing me?"

"No."

Actually, that was exactly it.

"Then why?"

"I have a bad ankle," I said. "Football injury."

Michael stared at me a moment. I bent forward and rubbed my left shin. He stared, then started walking again.

"Ow . . . ow!" I said, hobbling after him.

He stopped and watched me hobble forward.

"Why are you limping on the other one?" he asked.

Oops.

"I told you: bad ankles."

"You said 'ankle.'"

"Whatever," I said. "We need to talk."

"That's your shin, by the way."

"Quiet. We need to talk."

"About what?"

"What do you think?"

We'd reached the congestion of the main road. I followed Michael as he headed down the sidewalk and away from his neighborhood.

"Tell me about your dreams," I said.

"I don't know what—"

"La la la!" I put my fingers in my ears. "Tell me or I'm going to make a scene."

He stopped and stared. The noise from several packed lanes of speeding traffic washed over us. I felt like a water rat standing at the edge of a flooded river. I wondered what the other rat was thinking. Then I wondered whether he was going to try and push me in.

"Why are you doing this?" Michael demanded.

"So you'll talk."

"No, why are you trying to—"

"Because I'm tired of seeing you get pushed around," I said. "And I want to do something about it."

He stared.

I stared back.

He started walking again, and I sighed, thinking of the energy it would take to make a scene on the side of the road.

"Okay, Michael—"

"I can't really explain," he said.

"Explain what?" I asked.

Michael frowned at me. "The dreams."

"Yes, of course," I said.

He shook his head. "They wouldn't make any sense to you. I mean, there are *parts* that make sense, but most of them . . ." He trailed off, shaking his head. "Most are so arbitrary and surreal."

"I see."

Michael shot me a look.

"So what's the big deal?" I asked. "If they don't make sense and they're so arbital and surreal, why's your little friend back there so worked up?"

"*Arbital*?" Michael said, smiling just a little.

"You know what I mean," I said.

He nodded but didn't answer right away.

"Parts of them are pretty . . ."

I waited, but not for long. "Parts of them are pretty . . ." I prompted.

"Violent," he said.

"I get it. Keep going."

"I don't usually have dreams like that," he said. "And now I'm having them all the time."

"So who are you killing?" I asked.

He looked a little startled, but eventually said, "Jimmy thinks—"

"I don't care what Flap thinks," I said. "What do you think?"

"Flap?"

"Your buddy back in the bookstore," I explained. "What do *you* think?"

Michael sighed. "It's hard to explain," he said.

"You mentioned that."

"Because the characters in the dreams . . . they're supposed to be people—people I know—but they don't look anything like them."

"Michael, who?"

"Leonard."

"Shocking," I muttered.

"My stepfather."

"Your . . . Wait. Your who?"

"Stepfather," he said.

"Big gut?" I asked, holding my hand a few feet from my stomach.

"Yeah."

I congratulated myself for knowing something was up when he'd appeared on the other side of the door. I'd probably have nightmares about him too if I had to live with him. The thought of Gut wandering around the house in his boxers made me shudder.

"Oh my God," I said.

"What?"

"He doesn't wear briefs, does he?"

"What?"

"Never mind. Anybody else taking a beating in your head?" I asked.

Michael gave me a sour look but shook his head.

So, basically, Michael didn't like his stepfather, or the kids who pushed him around at school. Really abnormal, huh?

"Is that it?" I asked.

"Is what it?"

"That's what you're worried about?"

Michael hesitated. "Jimmy's worried," he said.

"Jimmy seems a little fussy."

"So dreams like that aren't important?" he asked.

"In my professional opinion? No."

"So I should just laugh about them in the morning?" he asked, starting to heat up.

"Easy now. I'm trying to help you, remember? I don't want to show up in your dreams tonight."

I thought it was a pretty funny line. Judging from Michael's face, he didn't share my opinion.

"Okay, relax. It was just a joke. Guess we need to work on your sense of humor, too."

"Why?"

"Never mind. Look, what if you weren't having the dreams anymore?" I said. "Would you still be all cramped-up?"

"All cramped-up?"

"That's my new thing—'all cramped-up.' Like it?"

Michael shrugged.

"Give it two weeks," I said. "It means all worked-up and hysterical."

"I'm not hysterical," he said.

"Whatever. I'm not going to argue about seamatics."

"Huh?"

"Seamatics."

"I think you mean semantics," Michael said.

"Stop talking," I said. "Anyway, I think I can help you." I thought for a minute. Convincing the entire school to leave him alone was a bit daunting. I needed to start smaller.

"We'll begin with Gut." Before he could say anything, I raised my hand. "'Gut' is your stepfather. You need to start thinking of him as 'Gut,' not as your stepfather."

"Why?"

"Because he's like a pet. He needs a name."

Michael stopped walking.

"Where are we going, anyway?" I asked. "We're never going to get there if you keep stopping."

"Why are you doing this?"

This again. I sighed. "Because you need my help, Michael . . . and I'm a wonderful, giving person."

Michael stared. Actually, he didn't just stare *at* me. He stared *into* me. I wasn't sure what he was looking for, or what he would find.

Maybe he'd just walk off again. And maybe this time I wouldn't follow him.

But then again, I'd already sacrificed a great deal of time, endured several difficult conversations with Michael, and narrowly avoided a pass from Flap. So losing Michael would be somewhat annoying.

And I _still_ hadn't gotten a "thank you" for rescuing him from Leonard.

But eventually, he gave in. I didn't see it—I felt it. It was like the air coming out of an inner tube, leaving Michael flat.

"Should I call him 'Gut' to his face?" Michael asked.

"Of course not," I said.

I turned, hoping Michael would follow. He did.

"And don't let it slip out, either," I said. "People like Gut aren't very observant, but they'll surprise you once in a while. Now let's go back to the bookstore. Jimmy's probably soiled his flap by now."

The bookstore wasn't far, but far enough for us to go over some of the basics.

"First of all, what's he do?" I asked.

"Who?"

"Gut, Michael. Pay attention."

"Watch TV."

"I mean for work. What's he do?"

"Construction."

"Shocking," I said. "Okay, works construction. Does he watch sports? Wait a minute. What am I saying? Of course he does."

"Football," said Michael. "And NASCAR."

"Fabulous. Favorite driver?"

"I don't know. I try not to watch when it's on."

"You might have to start," I said. "But for now, just find out who his favorite guy is."

"Why?"

"Because you're going to tell Gut he's gay."

Blank look.

"Gut?" Michael asked.

"His driver, Michael. We're going to plant a little something in his head," I said. "He'll say it isn't true, so you need to know what you're talking about. You'll need to know a couple of names. It's going to be something like . . . I don't know Vaughn Thomas was seen leaving a gay club at two in the morning . . . or maybe he made a pass at someone in the garage.

But you have to be specific, and you have to use the language. It has to *sound* plausible."

"Why?"

"Why does it have to sound plausible?"

"No, why am I doing it?"

"Because," I said, turning down the side street toward Flap's bookstore, "the first thing we need to do is throw him off balance. Do you think he's going to like hearing that his favorite driver is gay?"

"No," said Michael, smiling just a little.

"Of course not. And he'll say it's a lie and he'll say you're an idiot, but inside his little walnut brain, he'll wonder if it could be true," I said. "And then he's going to wonder if something's 'wrong' with him since he likes a gay driver."

We stopped by Flap's sign.

"And since he's not used to thinking," I said, "he's going to be just a little off balance. And when he is, we're going to push him a little more. And after that, we're going to push a little more. And once he's good and wobbly, you know what we're going to do?"

Michael shook his head.

"We're going to knock him over," I said with a wink.

I left Michael standing by the sign.

"Don't try anything tonight!" I said, getting into my car. "Just find out who his favorite driver is. Go online and learn something, okay?"

"Okay," Michael said.

I started the car and pulled away. I glanced in the rear view mirror and was pleased to see Michael still standing there, watching me coast down the street.

At a stop sign, I leaned over and opened the glove compartment, looking for a CD. I couldn't find it, but I did run across a black Sharpie.

I took it out and turned it over, considering.

I flirted briefly with the urge to modify Flap's sign, but tossed it back in the glove compartment.

Like I said, I don't really hate Flap, or his Flower Lady for that matter.

Sometimes, though, I think I'm too nice for my own good. I remember thinking that someday it was going to get me in trouble.

CHAPTER 6

Saturday.

I spent the morning doing a lot of nothing. Between the rigors of school and my newfound interest in Michael, I needed some downtime. I woke up late and watched a few episodes of *Pawn Stars* until hunger forced me out of my room.

I tromped down the stairs, but no one was in the kitchen.

I grabbed a bagel, managed to slice it in two without injuring myself, and topped it with as much cream cheese as possible. Opening the refrigerator to return the cream cheese, I decided to abscond with the entire orange juice carton—there wasn't much left anyway.

I retreated to my room, locking the door behind me.

I resumed my former position in bed, devoured my kill, and dozed in front of the TV for a while.

When I came to, I realized the plate had slipped from my lap and was now lying in three ragged pieces on the hardwood floor. I stared at it a while, but opted to clean it up later.

I took a shower and decided to visit Wanda.

Wanda is probably the only person in my life who's actually achieved "friend" status. Wanda's like a statue. She's tall and chiseled and looks like an Olympic sprinter. She's dark and fearless but reserved—her silence is like barbed wire. It's almost impossible to get through it and into her head.

No one can tell what is going on below the surface, and I only know what she wants me to know. Wanda thought she might end up playing poker for a living.

She didn't live that far from me, but in Northern Virginia, unless someone actually lives a couple doors down, you may be talking hours, not minutes, in the car. Going to Wanda's involved pulling out of our neighborhood onto a road that usually had about as much traffic as your average highway. After about fifty yards, you pushed your way down the ramp and onto the Beltway. And though it was only two or three exits, surviving the Beltway was always dicey.

After that, another clogged artery, then a couple of capillaries, and you were in her neighborhood.

I hadn't heard anyone downstairs and wondered if there was still a car in the garage. I shuffled down the stairs and peered into the kitchen.

No Mom, but it could mean she had the car. My eyes went to the hooks just above the writing desk.

Excellent. Her keys were still there.

Time to find her—or, actually, time to determine whether she was in the immediate vicinity.

"Mom?"

No response.

Helpful Hint: When calling for a parent in a situation where they might say "no," never raise your voice above normal conversation level. The intention is not actually to find them. (In other words, use your "inside voice," please.)

Rationale: You don't really want to find or speak to them. You just want a believable excuse when confronted later for not asking permission. I think it's called "possible deniability" or something. If you're that worried about it, go look it up. Here's an example:

"Why did you take the car without permission?"

"I didn't. I tried to find you, but you didn't answer."

"I was in the next room!"

Whisper: "I'm worried about your hearing loss."

I took my time wandering up the path that led to Wanda's front door.

Everything about Wanda's place is unusual and worth a second look. The flagstones are cut from some material I can't identify. The shrubs on either side of the path are either flawless replications or impeccably manicured living things. I stopped to inspect one.

I wasn't in a hurry. I hadn't called to see if she was home and didn't know where I'd go if she wasn't. I took a quick look, didn't see anyone nearby, and squatted beside the closest shrub. I still couldn't tell, but if they were fake, they were the greatest artificial plants ever produced.

I stood and dusted my hands, though it was more for show than to remove any real dirt.

Wanda's house is long and low. Large, spreading oaks protect it like a giant bird standing over her chick. There never seems to be any direct sunlight bearing down on the roof. There's a second, slightly higher roofline behind the first, but it can be difficult to see on an overcast day. I can't really tell you how big the house is. It's not something you can determine from the outside. Or from the inside, for that matter. I'd been inside several times, but only gotten past the front room once or twice. Like I said, Wanda doesn't let many people in.

I wandered up to the front door and rang the bell.

It was one of those bells you can't quite hear from the intruder's side of the door—the kind that leaves you thinking it might be broken, and maybe you should give it another push, just to make sure.

I waited uncomfortably, raised my hand to ring again, then tried to drop it when the door suddenly opened.

"I heard you," Wanda said. "You don't need to lean on it."

"I wasn't going to . . ." I started, but conceded the point to Wanda and slipped inside.

"Thanks for calling first," she said, walking to the middle of the room and settling into a slick black couch that faced the front door.

"You know you were waiting for me," I said.

Wanda snorted, sounding almost exactly like my mother. She stretched out across the length of the couch and propped herself up on an elbow, staring at something on the cushion. It might have been a tablet, but there was something about the shape or size that was off.

Wanda's house was filled with that sort of thing: items that were exotic, understated, and obviously expensive.

I sat across from her on a smaller couch (a love seat, or whatever they're called). Both seemed to be covered in black leather (either that or some new fiber only available to the military elite). My couch didn't have arms, which got me thinking. I pushed myself to the edge of it and leaned down in an attempt to look underneath. I couldn't spot any legs, so I just assumed the couch hovered.

There was something daunting about Wanda's "front room" that usually left me quiet and compliant. Medical waiting rooms could save themselves the hassle of unruly patients by studying it. It was spacious and spare, all its items streamlined and modern. The one exception was a tall piece of pottery, a vase that stood on a short, black box near the entrance to the kitchen. It could have been anywhere from three years old to three thousand. I was afraid to go near it, assuming I'd either crash into it or insult it by not averting my gaze.

All the furniture in the front room was angular and sharp. You had to be careful about how and where you moved or else risk a slash from the corner of an end table.

The front room's light was always muted. There was a row of windows behind the love seat that ran the length of the wall and ended at the front door.

There was an enchanted forest on the far side of the room. Exotic flowers grew in clumps across the ceiling.

Okay, so I made up a couple things, but I was getting a little disgusted with myself. I don't know why I tried to describe her house in the first place, but apparently I've just written the beginning of a book Michael will really enjoy.

"What are you doing?" I asked.

"Hmm?" she muttered, distracted.

"What's that thing in front of you?"

"You."

"Hilarious," I said. "The thing laying next to you—the device that seems to be getting more attention than I am?"

"What do you think it is?" she asked, looking up from her screen.

Wanda was stretched out on her couch like a lioness. The couch was long but not quite long enough. Her bare feet dangled off the edge. She turned off her device, then stood and stretched.

The curve of her body seemed to fill the room from ceiling to floor, a nearly perfect arc. It took me a minute to realize I was staring; I was definitely off my game.

She wandered toward the back of the room and into the kitchen. "Want something?" she said, her voice floating back to me from around a corner.

"No . . . thanks."

I sat on my hover-couch and folded my hands.

Looking around, I noticed a massive painting to my right. It was abstract, and the design was familiar, although it wasn't something I remembered from my last visit.

I stood and carefully slithered over to it. Having felt the burn of Wanda's sharp furniture once or twice, I refused to move at any speed above old-man shuffle.

I stopped a few feet from the painting.

"Is this real?" I asked.

I could see globs of paint that appeared to be three-dimensional, but wasn't quite sure I could trust my eyes.

I shot a furtive glance toward the kitchen, then brought a tentative finger toward a blob of red.

"You don't do that at the gallery, do you?"

The voice was so low and close that at first, I thought the painting was upbraiding me.

"No," I said, defensively tucking my arm against my side.

Wanda's mother emerged from a wormhole and stepped up beside me.

Her mother is just a bit taller than Wanda and, though not quite as muscular, somehow more imposing than her daughter.

"What do you think?" Mrs. W asked, nodding toward the painting.

I always called Wanda's mother Mrs. Wanda or Mrs. W. Can't really explain why. It just seemed to fit and she didn't seem to mind.

"Umm . . . it's real?" I tried.

She laughed.

"It better be. Do you like it?" she asked.

I turned back to the painting. I didn't need a second look to decide whether I liked it or not. It was hideous. But seeing Wanda's mother was an anomaly, and I needed a moment to get my head out of my ass.

"Of course I like it. It's very . . . it's . . . Actually, no . . . no, I don't," I finally admitted.

She smiled.

"Me, neither. But it's worth a lot."

"Yeah, I figured."

Wanda's voice cut in from the other side of the room.

"Going to work?"

"Mm-hm," her mom said.

"What time you coming back?"

Mrs. W shrugged.

"Can't tell me or don't feel like it?" Wanda asked.

Setting a tall drink on an end table that must have scuttled in behind her, Wanda folded herself back onto the couch.

"One of those," her mom said.

I don't know what her mom does for work. Wanda says she knows but can't tell me. I think she's lying. I've pressed Wanda on it a few times but haven't gotten anywhere.

"Headed for the pet shop?" I guessed.

Another smile from Mrs. W.

She slipped from my side, threading her way across the room and over to her daughter. "You can order dinner," she said, bending over Wanda to kiss her on the cheek.

Wanda had her device going again.

"You can stay for dinner if you like, Matthew," Mrs. W offered.

"Thanks."

"Not if he doesn't ask me first," Wanda said.

"You'd better watch yourself," her mom replied.

The change in her voice was subtle, but I suddenly found myself a bit more alert than I had been just a second ago.

"Yes, ma'am," Wanda said, quietly.

Her mother stood over her a moment, assessing, then leaned down and kissed her other cheek.

Wanda smiled.

To me, she said, "Wash your hands if you're planning on touching that painting again."

"Yes, ma'am," I said.

A quick smile and she slipped out the front door.

I stood in place a moment, then shuffled back over to my hover-couch. My leg brushed a coffee table on the way, opening a five-inch gash.

I fell into my seat, stared at my hands a minute, then looked up at Wanda.

"She gets to you, doesn't she?" Wanda said, smiling.

"Please," I said dismissively.

Wanda continued to stare. Wanda can see much farther into me than anyone else—it's a feeling I don't care for, but also one of the reasons I spend time with her. She's a worthy opponent. I haven't found a way past her barriers and definitely haven't discovered a way to beat her on a consistent basis. Spending time with someone like Wanda is good practice, not that I need a lot.

"I'd say she gets to you," I said.

"Different," Wanda said dismissively, eyes back on her device.

I raised my eyebrows but didn't press.

Not yet.

I cleared my throat and lowered my eyes just as hers lifted. I ran my palm across the fabric of the cushion. I frowned and brought my hand closer, staring at the palm. I shook my head—not much, but just enough.

"What?" she said.

"Nothing," I said, rubbing my palm against the leg of my pants.

"There's nothing on that couch," she said.

"Of course not," I said.

"Then why are you rubbing your leg?"

I didn't answer, but tried to look as if I might in just a moment. I gazed at the pottery, opened my mouth slightly, then closed it.

"Matthew?"

"Hey, what do you think of Michael?" I asked, nonchalantly.

"Michael?" she said.

"Yes, Michael."

"Michael who?"

I told her.

She lifted an eyebrow, then shrugged. "Don't know him."

I had to be careful. Too much push and she'd start asking questions. I feigned a renewed interest in the horrible painting.

"Why're you interested in Michael?" she asked.

I held up a finger, making her wait.

"Hey," she said, giving her cushion a *thump*.

Not yet.

"Better put that finger away," she said.

I complied, but did so slowly.

"Well?" she said.

"Well, what? Oh, right . . . Why am I interested in Michael?"

She nodded.

"Don't know. I was thinking about him the other day . . . thinking maybe there's some potential there."

"Potential?"

I nodded.

"For?"

"Not sure, yet . . . I mean, he's not a *bad* guy, right?"

Wanda shrugged.

"Seems to get more shit than he deserves," I said.

"And that's *your* battle?" she asked.

"*Battle*?" I said. "What are you talking about? What's in that drink, anyway?"

"You know what I mean," she said, voice low. I watched her poke the device with a little more force than was required.

"*Battle*," I repeated, as if I hadn't quite heard her right.

"Quit being such a pain in the ass," she said without looking up.

I gave myself a point. It's like the game I play with Mom. Getting Wanda to complain about my behavior is worth a point.

"Don't you think he could use a little help?" I asked.

"From you?"

Although it wasn't a bad comeback, it was easy, and the delivery was overdone. I chose not to award her a point.

"Yes, from me. I'm quite helpful."

Wanda stopped fiddling with her tablet. We stared at each other.

It was a draw, so I awarded myself another point.

"Good luck with that," she said.

"What do you mean?" I asked.

She didn't answer. Instead, she touched the screen in a few key places and put it to sleep. She set the tablet on the end table and stood up from the couch.

"I said—"

"I heard you," she said, stretching her arms toward the ceiling again.

"And?"

"And I'm not going to answer. You know what I mean."

"Not fair."

"Neither are you. I got to get ready, honey," she said, looking down at her drink.

"Are we going out to eat?" I asked.

"Nope."

"Oh . . . you're making something?"

"You need a ride home?" she asked.

"I just got here," I said.

"Should have called first."

"I'm supposed to stay for dinner."

"No, you're *allowed* to stay for dinner," she said. "I'm not going to be here for dinner."

"Where are we going?"

"I'm going to do some shopping."

"Okay," I said.

She raised her eyebrows. "You want to hang out while I try on clothes?"

"Sometimes it's important to get a second opinion," I said, giving her a meaningful look.

Based on Wanda's face, I awarded myself another point.

"Doing anything tonight?" I asked.

"Got a poker game."

"Can I come?"

"You know how to play poker?"

"Yes."

"I don't think so."

"You don't know everything about me," I said.

She smiled. "I know one thing: You're going to get yourself in trouble if you start fooling with Michael and messing in his business."

"Michael?" I said. "Michael who?"

"I got to get going," she said again but didn't leave. "You want anything to eat?"

"Yes."

"You know where the kitchen is."

She turned and walked down the hall. I gave her a point for not looking back.

I sat on the hover couch and reviewed my performance while I waited. Although the start had been a bit shaky, I'd made a nice recovery. In fact, it was such a nice recovery, I decided to give myself the win.

As I gazed at a corner of the room, Michael floated back into my head. Trailing along after him like a banner was Wanda's comment about getting involved in his "battles."

I shook my head.

If I could score a win over Wanda on her home field, winning a few battles for Michael was nothing. I might even put in my second-stringers.

They could use the playing time.

CHaPTeR 7

The rest of Saturday and all of Sunday were so boring I was almost glad to get to school Monday morning. I decided to look for Michael, but he wasn't in the cafeteria. Instead, he was standing by my locker, looking all flushed and out of breath.

"You're not going to tell me about some computer game, are you?" I said.

"What? No . . . I was going to tell you about the weekend."

"Oh, good," I said. "What's up?"

He hesitated, looking confused.

"I wanted to . . ."

"Did you get lucky?" I asked.

"I . . . no . . . *What*?"

"Nothing. Sorry, go ahead."

Michael cleared his throat, paused, and said, "I did that thing we talked about. Remember?"

"The racing thing?" I asked, a little surprised.

He nodded, regaining some of the geek flush he'd lost. He let his backpack slide off his shoulder and onto the floor. He squatted down beside it and began to rummage through. It took him a while, but he finally closed it up and slung it back into place.

"What's that?" I asked.

Michael held a spiral notebook in one hand.

"My research," he said, handing me the book.

My jaw dropped as I flipped through. There must have been fifteen pages of notes. There were diagrams—little clouds with names inside floating around the page and different-colored lines linking one cloud to another.

"What *is* this?" I asked, pointing to the clouds.

"Oh, that's just something to help me remember different teams and owners."

"*Just something*, huh?"

Michael looked pleased. "Actually, it's kind of interesting the way some drivers—"

I held up a hand. "That's okay. I appreciate the thought, but no thank you."

I skimmed through a few more pages and handed the notebook back.

"Excellent," I said. "So now you know everything in the world about racing."

"Is it too much?"

"It's fine. Don't worry about it."

He looked uncomfortable.

"What?" I asked.

"I told him."

"Told who?"

"My stepfather. I told him about the rumor."

I closed my eyes. "Michael, this isn't going to work if you don't follow my instructions."

"I know. I'm sorry. But he was watching racing last night and I thought—"

"You *thought* . . . ?"

"I wanted to . . . It seemed like a good opportunity."

"Fine," I said. "Just tell me what happened."

Michael smiled. He really wasn't such a strange looking kid when he smiled.

"So I told him there was this rumor—"

I held up a hand. "Why are you starting at the end?" I said.

His face began to fall.

"And you can't get upset when I give you constructive criticism, Michael. It's just a part of the lesson plan."

Michael nodded.

"Where'd we leave off?" I asked.

"Leave off?"

"Where were we last time I saw you?" I said.

"I was . . ."

"Oh, yeah. At the bookstore, right? I left you at Jimmy Flap's . . . Friday? Friday. That's where you should start."

"Okay, well, I did some research at Jimmy's—"

"Was he happy to see you?" I said.

"I guess."

I sighed. "It's the details that make a good story, Michael. So you walk back into Flap's and he's beside himself, of course."

"He's what?"

"Probably started fussing over you the minute you walked through the door," I said. "'Michael, thank God! Where have you been? Was Woodrow mean to you?'"

It took Michael a second.

"I'm not sure I . . . Why did your voice—?"

"I was pretending to be Flap," I said. "Pretty good, huh? Uncanny, even."

"Uh . . ."

"Never mind. Sense of humor comes later," I said. "So you walk into Flap's, he's hysterical for a while. Then what?"

"I did some research," he said, still a little uncertain.

"That?" I asked, pointing to the notebook.

He nodded.

"At Flap's? He's got a section on racing?"

"No. I used his computer."

"Oh."

"Actually, it was hard to concentrate," he said. "Jimmy kept asking me where we'd been and when I was going to call his doctor."

"Did he wonder what you were doing?" I asked.

"He couldn't figure out why I was looking at racing stuff."

"What did you tell him?"

"School project."

"Not bad," I said. "So you did your research Friday. When did you drop the rumor on Gut?"

"Last night."

"That's right. You said that . . . Wait."

"What?" he asked.

"I thought you didn't know who his favorite driver was."

"I asked my mom."

I didn't say anything for a second, then nodded slowly. "Not bad," I said, giving him a little pat on the shoulder. He winced at first, but accepted the pat with a weak smile.

"So where were you guys?" I asked.

"Watching TV."

"Excellent. What was he wearing?"

"Huh?"

"What was he wearing? Details, Michael!"

"A t-shirt, I think . . . and pants," he said.

"Did the t-shirt have sleeves?"

"Yes."

"Damn it."

"But he was watching racing," Michael said. "Well, actually, it wasn't a race. It was a weekly wrap-up thing. The next big race isn't until—"

I held up my hand. "Did you sit down and watch with him?" I asked.

"Yes."

"Confused him, didn't you?"

Michael smiled. "Yeah . . . He said, 'I'm not turning it.'"

I waited. Then, finally: "And?!"

"Oh . . . and I said, 'Good. I want to see the highlights.'"

"Well-played, sir!" I said, clapping him on the shoulder.

This time he grinned.

"Continue," I said.

"Well, he stared at me, but I pretended like I was interested in the show . . ."

Michael kept talking. I got the story out of him, but wasn't impressed with the presentation, so I've decided to recreate the scene myself.

After all, I tell a *much* better story.

Michael slumped down on the filthy couch next to his stepfather.

"I ain't changin' it," Gut growled from behind his lit cigarette.

"Good," Michael fired back. "I want to see the racing."

Gut's head whipped around. He turned his icy stare on Michael. Michael kept his eyes locked on the dusty, flickering television screen.

"What did you say?" Gut asked dangerously.

"I said I want to watch the racing," Michael said.

"Since when do you like racing?" Gut demanded.

"Always have."

"You know there's no elves or dragons in racin', right?" Gut said with a sneer.

"I've been watching for a long time," said Michael, ignoring Gut's humorous but nasty remark.

Gut grunted like a pig. "Like hell you have," he said. "Who's your favorite driver?"

"Don James," said Michael without missing a beat.

Gut shifted positions to get a better look at his hated stepson.

"You like Don James?" he said, incredulously.

Michael nodded, his eyes locked on the unholy glow of the television. "He's consistent."

"What's his number?" Gut said.

"Four."

Gut continued to stare in speechless amazement.

"You like Ricky Earl, don't you?" Michael ventured casually.

"Yeah. So what?"

"He's gay, you know."

Gut's cigarette dropped from his bottom lip to the couch below. He jumped up, cursing, plucked the cigarette from between the couch cushions, and angrily stabbed it out in a nearby ashtray.

"What did you just say?" he said, menacingly.

"Maybe he's not," Michael said, "but if you're leaving Killers at two in the morning with a 'friend' you just met . . ."

Gut swore.

"Maybe he's not," Michael said. "I'm just surprised you hadn't heard yet."

"That's a bunch of shit."

"I heard he might pull out of the SteelWheel 500," Michael said, turning back to the TV.

"He's not racing 'cause he's got a bad leg," Gut said.

"Well, that's what his people are saying," Michael said quietly.

"What the hell's that supposed to mean?!"

"It just seems strange that, all of a sudden, his leg's giving him trouble again," said Michael. "It's been almost a year since the crash."

Gut was speechless. Michael stood.

"Hey, let me know if they say anything about Ricky Earl," Michael said over his shoulder, leaving Gut on the couch to stew in a haze of cigarette smoke and armpit funk.

***

"So wait a minute," I said. "Is this guy really pulling out of the Steel . . . this Steel thingy?"

"Excuse me." A small, owlish kid was staring up at me.

"Yes?" I demanded.

"My . . . I need to . . ." he stammered, pointing at something behind me.

"His locker," Michael said.

"Oh." I grudgingly stepped to one side. "Anyway," I said, shaking my head, "is this guy really pulling out of the Steel—"

"SteelWheel 500," Michael said. "It's the next big race."

"And he's pulling out because of his leg?"

"He injured it in a crash about a year ago, but he re-injured it, so he's going to have another procedure."

"But he's really pulling out?"

Michael nodded.

"Do you know how incredible this is?" I asked.

Michael smiled.

"It's unbelievable," I said. "So he's really pulling out? And it was on the news?"

Michael nodded.

I shook my head in disbelief and turned to the owlish kid next to me who was trying to open his locker.

"Can you believe this shit?" I said.

"What?" he asked, looking frightened.

I turned back to Michael. "I'm a genius, Michael. Do you know that?"

"Yeah . . . I guess."

"No, there's no guessing involved, Michael. I am," I said. "This is perfect. I mean, just planting the rumor would have worked, but this guy pulling out is such a bonus. It sounds completely believable now."

"I put them together," Michael said quietly, looking down at the tiles.

"What?"

"I put them together," he said.

"Put what together?"

"Never mind," he said.

"Don't you 'never mind' me," I said. "You put what together?"

"The thing about the driver pulling out. I put it together with the rumor we made up."

"The rumor *I* made up."

"Fine."

I almost launched into a lecture about our roles but, just in time, I remembered who I was dealing with. This was Michael, not Wanda or someone with a higher skill set. An overly long "mean" look would be more than enough to put him in his place.

And besides, this whole thing was supposed to be about Michael. I could take the credit later, perhaps when I write my autobiography.

It was hard, but I finally managed to give him a pat on the head. Not a real one, of course. I'd just washed my hands.

"Well, you did do a lot of research," I said.

Michael looked up from the tiles.

"And the timing was perfect," I added.

Michael regained a bit of his earlier flush.

"We're both geniuses, or genii, or whatever the word is."

Michael opened his mouth. I held up a hand.

"I don't really want to know, Michael."

"Oh, okay."

"Now," I said, "it's time to think about Stage Two."

The bell rang. We automatically started walking down the hall.

"Stage Two's going to be a little different than Stage One," I said. "It's—which way are you going?" I asked.

Michael pointed.

"Me, too," I said with a nod. We headed down the hall together. "Keep talking to him about racing," I said. "We want him thinking about the rumor as much as possible. But don't just walk up and say, 'So, heard anything about your gay driver?' Start talking about the next race or some other guy, or how great some car is. You know what I mean?"

Michael nodded.

"Don't worry. Whenever racing comes up, you'd better believe he's going to start thinking about his driver. But, Stage Two . . . Stage Two has to be different."

"Why?"

"Balance," I said. "We've got to expand our focus. We need to attack everything that makes Gut, Gut."

"And then we push him over?" Michael asked.

"You're looking forward to that, aren't you?"

"Yes."

We weren't far from Astronomy.

"I'm going to think about Stage Two during my study block," I said, nodding toward the classroom.

"Isn't that Astronomy?" Michael asked.

"I don't like Astronomy anymore. I do other things in here."

I had signed up for Astronomy thinking we'd get to go on lots of field trips to the planetarium and look at stars, but apparently, astronomers don't look at the sky anymore. They just do math problems and listen to physics lectures.

"Okay, well . . . should I . . ."

"Should you what?"

"Should I call or something?"

"Call who?"

"Call you . . . so we can talk about the next stage."

"You look better with a little color," I said, pointing to his cheeks. Michael was very red. "You should try a little rouge once in a while."

"What?"

"Never mind. Just say, 'See you later.'"

"Okay, see you later."

"No calls, please, unless it's an emergency. I don't like the phone. I'll find you when I'm ready for Stage Two," I said.

Turning to go, I almost plowed into Dennis. Dennis lives down the street from me. When we were kids, he used to come to my house once in a while, until his mom found out about the Dennis Game, which involved sticking Dennis in a tomato cage and sliding in as many tomato stakes as possible. Eventually, he'd cry, and my mom would come running.

These days, we say "Hey" when I'm unable to avoid him in the neighborhood and occasionally exchange forced small talk when I inadvertently find myself walking next to him in-between classes. By this point, he'd probably have forgotten all about it, except that, on the rare occasions our social paths do cross, I like to bring it up when he's chatting with a nice young lady.

"Dude, that was *Michael*," Dennis whispered.

"Yep."

"What the hell?"

Something came to me as we walked. Not Stage Two. More like Stage One and a Half.

"Michael's a badass," I said.

"What?!"

"Didn't you hear?" I said. "He got jumped last night and beat the shit out of three guys."

"No way."

"Nathan was there," I said.

I don't know Nathan very well, but he's the kind of guy who always seems to either witness or participate in any/all events of interest.

"He saw it?"

I gave Dennis a few more vague details, then headed for my seat. Even though I was still working on the home front, why not plant a few seeds for the upcoming school campaign?

I sat in Astronomy and considered Stage Two. People like Gut aren't very complex; their world is black and white and no in-between (and I'm not talking about the racial stuff). For example, I can already tell you that Gut likes classic rock. I can also tell you what he thinks of music that isn't classic rock. Gut loves his Chevy or Ford or whatever "American" car he drives.

Gut knows what men do and what women do and gets *very* uncomfortable when somebody moves across the line. Take employment, for instance. Men lift things. Women cut hair. Men fix things. Women care for children. Computers are baffling. Men who work with computers are suspect and, at the very least, probably effeminate.

It's fairly easy to knock someone like Gut off-balance, but it's also easy to make him angry. He's the statue and we have the crowbars. Tip him a little too soon, however, and he might topple backwards on you.

I took out my notebook. Michael needed to develop a sudden interest in classic rock—Boston, Eric Clapton, Steve Miller. Michael needed to infringe on Gut's territory a bit more.

But it was awfully hard to think with the teacher yammering away. I propped my book up in front of me and put my head on the desk. I'm guessing that most social workers aren't expected to perform their duties while fighting off the side effects of an Astronomy lecture. (There are quite a few, but the explosive diarrhea is the worst.)

Oh . . . and Michael needed a nickname. Spike . . . the Hammer . . . something completely inappropriate.

For some reason, "Ducky" popped into my head, and I knew I was falling asleep.

I wondered when my teacher would come out of her trance and realize half the class was asleep. Probably just before she retired. That's what they should give people who can't sleep—an Astronomy lecture. I let go and began to float, hoping I wouldn't end up in a puddle of drool upon my return.

Chapter 8

Tuesday came and I decided I needed a day without any Michael work. I deserved one after the racing victory. I passed Michael once, on my way to lunch, and thankfully he wasn't pinned up against a locker. He flushed and smiled when he saw me and held up a hand. I gave him a serious nod, just to see what he would do. The hand dropped back to his side. He looked perplexed.

I decided to make an in-home visit after school on Wednesday. Michael and I needed a strategy session and Mom said she'd be working from home Wednesday. That was kind of weird—Mom rarely worked from home, and this was the third time in two weeks—but I'm smart enough not to ask questions when things go my way. I decided not to tell Michael about the strategy session. I didn't want him cleaning up or chasing family out of the living room.

On Wednesday afternoon, after hanging out a little after the last bell with Jack and a couple other kids—no sense in getting to Michael's house before he did—I headed our for Michael's.

I did some sightseeing on the way. I decided that some of the neighborhood houses weren't *that* bad. There only seemed to be four different styles of house, though: one-level, two-level, smaller one-level, and smaller two-level.

Most of the bricks were a shade I'd call "exhausted pink" and may have been "pre-owned" bricks the developer got on sale. Most looked like they might fall apart if you ran a hard finger over them.

I know I've mentioned a career in law enforcement as well as social work, but pursuing either would probably be a slap in the face to the architectural community. I clearly have a gift. However, both architects and social workers spend a lot of time in school, and I'm just not prepared to do that.

Even with the pre-owned brick façade, most of the houses weren't awful. But Michael's block—there just wasn't any way around it. They were bad. I wondered if they'd ever looked new. Did everyone in the neighborhood start junking-up their houses at the same time, or did it start with one guy who just didn't care? Maybe it was a couple families that didn't care. Then everybody else said, "Well, if they don't care, we don't either."

Or maybe the guys that built them didn't care. Maybe they left things half-finished. Or maybe they left all their crap around when they were done. But how come not one person cared about the rusty swing set slowly falling in on itself, or the flock of empty snack bags cartwheeling across the front yard? Or how come one person didn't say, "You know what? I'm never going to use all these old engine parts. Think I'll take them to the dump or something."

Standing at the end of Michael's driveway, I shook my head, trying to clear it. Time to focus on Gut, not the houses.

As I worked my way up the driveway, I could hear music coming from a window. I stopped.

Sounded like classical music.

Oh well, I thought. *I suppose it's one way to piss Gut off.* I pounded on the storm door and waited.

Eventually, my old buddy wandered up.

"Yeah?" he said.

Still no sleeveless t-shirt. *Maybe I could leave a three-pack on the stoop one night?*

"Michael around?" I asked.

"Yeah."

He stepped away from the door and I let myself in. Another stroke of inspiration hit me as the screen door slammed back into place.

"Hey, did Michael tell you?" I asked.

"Tell me what?"

"The coach wants him to play football next year."

Blank look from Gut.

"I said, 'The coach wants him to play football next—'"

"I heard you the first time, and it didn't make sense then, either. Why?"

"Why what?"

"Why would they want Michael on the team?"

"Coach wants him to play quarterback or something," I said. "Saw him throw in gym."

"Bullshit."

I had reached too high. "What do you mean?" I asked.

"There ain't no way they want Michael to throw the ball. He'd get killed."

"I didn't say 'throw.' I said 'kick.'"

"You said quarterback."

"I meant kicker."

"Oh, kicker," he said.

"Not bad, huh?"

Gut shrugged. "Kicker's just a soccer player with a helmet."

So much for that.

"So can I see him or what?"

"Yep. Back that way," Gut said, pointing down the hall.

The house smelled like a musty, old, chain-smoking dog. The carpets were thin, and like the bricks outside, everything inside had a washed-out look, as if all of it had been left in the sun way too long.

The living room floor was covered in a shade that might have passed for chocolate brown at one point, but now deserved a more accurate title, like putrid brown.

The carpet that graced the hallway was green—the pea variety of green. It made me wonder if the colors had been selected as a joke. Or perhaps while drunk, or maybe as an act of revenge.

Gut worked his way back to the couch and plopped down in front of the TV. Sports highlights.

"Racing news?" I asked.

"After this," he said, glancing up at me.

I stared at the TV like I was trying to remember something.

"What?" he said.

"I don't know," I said. "Thought I heard something about racing the other day."

"What do you mean?"

I shook my head. "I can't remember. It was something weird, though."

"Ain't nothing weird going on," he said.

"No, it was something strange. I'm pretty sure."

"Must've been something else," he mumbled.

I risked a quick glance. He was scowling at the TV.

Perfect.

I headed down the hall. It was narrow and dim but peppered with photographs—family pictures, I guessed—scattered across the wall, as if every once in a while, someone stopped to look, got depressed, and decided to add another picture.

Most of the pictures appeared to be school photos, and very few looked like Michael. The clothes in the photos had been atrocious even when they were in fashion. Hair was plastered to heads. Smiles were missing teeth. But I suppose missing teeth is somewhat natural. All kids lose teeth at some point, right?

Some of the pictures featured old people, and several were done in the school picture/mug shot-style the family seemed to favor. Maybe Grandma and Grandpa had visited the school photographer on his day off. One of the old ladies looked nice, in a grandmotherly way, but most of the grandpas looked like mean old bastards who wouldn't need much provocation to come down off the wall and give you a "whuppin."

Mom hires a photographer to come to our house when it's time for another picture. Usually, we end up outside in the backyard next to the water fountain or flowering bush. Dad and I receive instructions from Mom about dress, and the photographer usually orders us into ridiculous positions before agreeing to release us.

In Michael's house, there were a few outdoor shots in addition to the portraits, but most involved "casual" attire, flimsy folding chairs, and at least one beer per participant.

Michael's door was closed. I raised my hand to knock but decided to barge in instead. I was disappointed when I did. Michael wasn't doing anything weird. He was in a chair, leaning back and reading a book. I stood there for a minute, waiting for him to notice me.

Michael's room was small, tidy, and little-old-man like. His books were either in bookcases or stacked in neat piles on the floor. It wasn't hard to imagine Flap stopping by to reorganize the shelves or play a quick game of *Magic*.

The computer in the center of his desk seemed out of place. It looked new, and so far, it was the nicest object in the house. I was surprised it wasn't on display in the living room.

His bed was made (good boy, Michael!). It was narrow and way too small for him, but there weren't any stuffed animals propped up against the pillows, and I didn't see any action figures engaged in mortal combat.

There was a small poster above the desk, but was it someone cool? Of course not. It was a picture of a wrinkled old man wearing a diaper and holding a giant walking stick.

There were a few other posters near his bed—of star clusters, galaxies, and planets. And above the stereo (which, despite looking to be about fifty years old, was the source of the classical music) was another old man, but this one, at least, appeared to be wearing pants.

Michael finally came out of his book long enough to notice there was someone in his doorway. I stepped in and closed the door behind me. I approached the stereo, killed the classical, and fiddled with a button or two until I found a classic rock station. It didn't take long.

"What are you doing?" he asked.

"Stage Two."

I sat down on his bed. There was a Bible on the nightstand beside me. I held it up and raised my eyebrows.

Michael shrugged. His eyes went to the paperback in his lap. "I'm not a fundamentalist," he said.

"And that means?"

"I don't believe in the literal truth of the Bible."

"Keep going," I said, rolling a hand as if trying to scoop the air closer to my chest.

"I don't believe that all the passages were divinely inspired."

We stared at each other.

"So it *is* science-fiction," I said.

"No," Michael said. "I think a lot of it came from God."

I rolled my hand again.

"But I think some passages were changed."

"By who?"

"Priests. Monks," he said. "They were the only ones who could make copies of the Bible, back before the printing press. I'm sure they changed some of the passages or left some things out."

"Why?"

"To suit the leaders of the Church. To match their agenda."

So Michael was a conspiracy guy.

"Michael, were you abducted by aliens?" I asked, concerned.

Michael tried to study his carpet.

"Okay, relax! I'm sorry I said anything," I said. "You really need to get used to someone giving you a hard time once in a while. It doesn't always mean they hate you."

Michael brought his head back up. "I just think there have to be pieces of the Bible that were left out or changed," he said. "Pieces the church leaders thought weren't meant for everyone."

"So why do you have a Bible in here?"

"I didn't say it was *entirely* corrupt."

I stared.

"There's some beautiful writing in the Bible," said Michael, "And some beautiful ideas."

"Who's the naked guy?" I asked, pointing to the picture above his desk.

"Gandhi."

I didn't say anything.

"He was a leader in India, back when they were ruled by the British."

"Believe it or not, Michael, I've actually heard the name. I'm wondering why he's on your wall."

"He was a great man. He practiced nonviolent civil disobedience."

"Which means . . .?"

"Not fighting. Just refusing to cooperate."

I shrugged, which Michael interpreted as a request for more information.

"Nonviolent civil disobedience," he began. "Let's say you didn't think it was fair that the government made you carry a driver's license, and a police officer pulled you over for driving too fast. What would you do if he asked for your license?"

"Punch him in the mouth."

"No. And that was exactly Gandhi's point," he said, beginning to flush.

"Michael, I was—"

"Gandhi taught *nonviolent* disobedience. So he would probably say that you should tell the cop that you don't have one because you don't think it's a just law. And when the cop tries to arrest you . . ."

"I don't think they'd arrest you for—"

". . . you should just go with him. You should let him arrest you and not put up a struggle. And if everybody did that, without fighting, then they wouldn't be able to hold everyone. The prisons would fill up, and they'd run out of room. Then they'd have to change the law."

I almost told him it wouldn't work. I figured Michael was getting carried away and starting to exaggerate, but decided against it. If he wanted to believe in this sort of thing, fine. Besides, watching him get all worked up was kind of entertaining.

"So it worked for No Pants there?" I asked, pointing at Gandhi.

"He changed a whole country. He beat one of the strongest armies in the world by not fighting back."

Unfortunately, it was like playing with a little kid—I'd gotten him overexcited, and now I needed to bring him back or I was in for an extended lecture.

"Amazing," I said. "Let's talk about Stage Two. You need to start listening to classic rock."

Michael frowned.

"Loud enough so Gut can hear it in the living room."

"Why?"

"Does Gut listen to classic rock?" I asked.

"Yes."

"Do you think he'd like it if you did too?"

"I don't know."

"What if he had to come down the hall and tell you to turn it down?"

Michael wasn't following.

"Don't you think he'd be a little conflicted?" I said. "Telling you to turn down music he likes?"

"Maybe."

Something outside the window caught my attention—a woman picking her way up the driveway. She was small and thin and immediately reminded me of some kind of rodent. That's another theory of mine, by the way. Physically, everyone in the world looks like one of six animals: fish, bird, rat, pig, bear, or horse. Try it sometime.

"Who's that?"

"My mom," he muttered.

Wow.

Michael and Mom definitely looked like they both belonged to the rat family. Something about the nose and mouth. They weren't so startling on Michael, but on Mom they were disturbing.

"Let's go meet her," I said, slipping out of his room and down the hall. Michael tried to say something, but I ignored him. On my way past Gut, I said, "They get to that story yet?"

"What story?"

"The weird one I was telling you about," I said. "The one I couldn't remember."

"Ain't no story," he said, scowling at the TV. He sounded like a toddler: *I'm not gonna take a nap!*

I let him sulk and found my way to the kitchen. Michael's mom was unloading groceries.

"Mrs. . . . ?" I almost said "Mrs. Rat," but stopped myself just in time.

She looked at me as if I'd threatened to kick her. "Yes?"

"I'm Michael's friend Matthew," I said, just as Michael rounded the corner.

"Oh . . . hello," she said.

"Did you get waffles?" Gut asked from the couch.

"Would you like some help putting those away?" I asked.

She stopped for a second, as if trying to remember something. "No. Thank you."

"Michael wanted me to meet you," I said, smiling.

"Did you get waffles?" Gut asked again, louder this time.

"Yes!" she called.

"Likes his waffles, doesn't he?" I said.

"Yes," Mom said.

"Okay, well, you probably need to go," Michael said, trying to shoo me out the door.

"No, I'm fine," I said. I wasn't about to let Michael chase me away. When would I get another chance to experience the whole family together? "Are you just getting home from work?"

"Yes," she said, busy putting cans into cabinets.

"Where do you work?"

"At the hospital," Michael said.

"Are you a nurse?" I asked.

"Medical records," Michael said.

"I didn't know you were a ventriloquist, Michael."

Mom and son gave me the same baffled look.

Okay, so his looks and *sense of humor came from Mom.*

"We're out of butter," Gut said. He'd managed to pry himself off the couch.

Mom glanced at him. "I wish you'd told me that this morning," she said to the head of lettuce on the counter.

"Forgot," Gut said, beginning to pick his teeth.

"Toothpick?" I offered.

Gut shook his head.

"Okay, well . . ." Michael began.

"Did you tell her yet, Michael?" I said, interrupting.

"Tell me what?" she asked, alarmed.

Michael stared at me.

"Fine, I'll tell her. Your son is incredibly modest," I said. "They want Michael to play football."

Gut snorted.

"Who does?" She sounded worried.

"The school. Michael's not sure he wants to do it, but still—"

"Them elves he's always fightin' might not like it," said Gut. "Might attack the house or something."

"Did you play football in high school?" I asked Gut before Michael could respond.

"Fullback," Gut grunted. "I didn't just run around kickin' balls like a little—"

Mom looked at Gut, then said, "Michael doesn't really like team sports."

"Mom!" Michael said.

"Well, you don't," she said, then went back to her groceries.

"Michael's one of them loner guys you hear about on TV," Gut said.

"Kind of like a race car driver," I said.

"What?"

"Kind of like a driver."

"Nah," said Gut. "They got a whole pit crew to work with."

"But when they're racing, I mean. When they're out there on the track all by themselves. Must get kind of lonely."

"What do you mean?" Gut asked, hairy eyebrows knitting together.

"Good thing they have those pretty girlfriends . . . or whatever."

"*Whatever*?" he repeated.

"You know—girlfriends, families . . . significant others."

Gut grunted and looked away.

"So, you ready to go?" I asked Michael.

He nodded.

"Nice to meet you," I said to Michael's mom.

"You, too," she said.

Yeah, right.

"You'll let me know if you hear that story?" I asked as Gut shuffled back toward the couch.

"Uh-huh," he said, absently.

Michael and I headed out. I shook my head on the way down the stairs.

"What?" Michael asked.

"Going to be a little harder than I thought," I said.

"Why?"

"You're not going to get much help from Mom."

Michael was quiet.

"Michael, where's your dad?" I said.

He didn't answer right away. I took a quick peek and figured I was in for a battle, but before I could begin the assault, he said, "Baltimore."

"Really?"

He nodded.

"Michael, that's only, like, forty minutes away. Do you ever see him?"

A headshake.

"Why not?"

I looked over when I didn't get an answer.

Michael's eyes were on the ground and his jaw was set. He looked like he was preparing for a dental procedure.

"So, when was the last time you saw him?" I said.

"I'm not sure," said Michael. "It's been a while."

"Days? Weeks?"

"Years. Since I was little."

"Why?"

We hit the busy intersection. Michael finally shrugged. "He left us," he said. "Why should I go see him?"

"Aren't you curious?"

"He's a drunk."

That was a pretty good reason. *But wait a minute,* I thought. *How would he know?*

"Are you sure?" I asked.

"What do you mean?"

"Your mom probably doesn't talk about your dad much, does she?"

"Not really. Not unless I push," he said.

"So how do you know?"

"How do I know *what*?"

"How do you know she's telling you the truth?"

Michael hesitated.

"Why doesn't he try to see me?" he asked.

"Maybe he's not allowed," I said. "Maybe there's a court order or something."

Michael was quiet. I couldn't believe he hadn't thought of this before. "But wouldn't he try anyway?" he asked.

"Try what?"

"Try to see me? To tell me what was going on?"

"I don't know, Michael."

I suddenly realized we'd turned off the main road. We were on our way to Flap's bookstore. I began to wonder how many times a week Michael ended up at Flap's.

It was like a cigarette, or a security blanket. After every argument with Gut, or a bad day at school, Michael headed for the store. It was a habit he needed to break. He couldn't keep running to the bookstore every time someone hurt his feelings. He needed to start standing up for himself, and he definitely needed to stop believing everything people fed him.

"*Your father's a drunk.*" "*You need to talk to someone about your dreams.*"

Michael needed to see his real dad and draw his own conclusions.

I stopped.

"Michael, what day is it?"

"Uh . . . Wednesday, I think."

"What are you doing this weekend?"

I waited for him to flip through his mental calendar.

"Big plans?" I asked, getting impatient.

"No . . . I can't think of anything."

"Well, if you can clear a couple hours, I think we should take a little road trip."

"We should?"

I nodded.

"Wait. You mean you want to go to—?"

"Yep."

"But I don't know where he lives."

"You know his name, don't you?"

"Yeah."

I took Michael by the shoulders and turned him back toward the main road, away from the bookstore.

"What are you doing?" he asked.

"You're going back home," I said. "I need you to use that lovely computer in your room and find out where your father lives."

Michael stared at me, then glanced over his shoulder toward the bookstore. *Probably hoping Flap will open the door and wave him over,* I thought. But I also had a feeling that seeing his father was, in fact, something he wanted, so I waited patiently, even though I wanted to shake him.

"What if he's not there this weekend?" Michael finally asked.

"We'll leave a note and show up some other day," I said. "At least you'll know how to get there."

"He probably won't be there," Michael said.

"You're probably right," I said. "We'll just head up, leave a note, and come back down. It'll take like an hour."

Michael seemed to like this. He took a few steps toward home.

"There's a bookstore in Baltimore I'd like to visit," he said.

"Sure. Road trips are supposed to be crazy like that."

"It's a used bookstore," he explained. "They have a lot of out-of-print books."

"Uh-huh."

"It's really cool. They specialize in rare and hard-to-find science-fiction and fantasy."

I led Michael back to his house. It was like steering a senile old man back to the safety of the nursing home. He told me more about the bookstore. I nodded and said things like, "Oh, wow, that sounds cool."

When I left him near the side door, he was still talking about it. Apparently, it was run by elves, filled with treasure, and served as the entrance to an alternate universe (much like Wanda's house). Or at least that's what I think he said—I wasn't really listening.

I remember debating my long-term career plans on the drive back to school. Obviously, I was a highly desirable candidate for any of the premier schools of social work, as well as a top architectural prospect. Not to mention the letter of intent the police department was badgering me to sign.

Lying in bed that evening, I envisioned the happy reunion I'd arranged for the weekend. I wondered how emotional it would get. I wasn't big on crying, and I definitely didn't want anyone hugging me. It would kind of put a damper on things. Hopefully, I'd be safe if I stood to one side and held up a hand if anybody got too close.

"I'm sorry, I'm a professional. I'm not at liberty to get physically involved with my clients."

Strange, though, how things don't always turn out like they're supposed to.

CHAPTER 9

With the exception of my home visit on Wednesday and the impending road trip, the week was pretty uneventful. And as an added bonus, the rumor I'd started about Michael was beginning to make some good headway.

"Did you hear about your little buddy, Michael?" Jack asked Thursday at lunch.

"Michael? What about him?" I asked, suddenly pulled back into the present. Jack had been going on and on about some love interest (although "love" wasn't the right word).

"He got in a fight. Downtown. At the Crossbow."

"He what?" I said, trying to look surprised. "What the hell was Michael doing at the Crossbow?"

Jack shrugged. "I don't know, but apparently he beat the crap out of three guys."

"Get out," I said.

"Seriously," Jack said, like he was an eyewitness.

"Please," I said. "Michael? You're telling me he was just hanging out in D.C. and gets into a big fight? Where'd you hear this shit?"

"Nathan."

"Nathan," I said, grimacing. "Nathan's everywhere, isn't he?"

"What do you mean?"

"He's a little busybody. Ever notice how Nathan's *always* right in the middle of everything?"

"I guess." Jack shrugged.

He was quiet for a while, considering. I started to worry that I'd overplayed my hand when Jack asked, "Anything going on this weekend?"

"No idea," I said. I told him to give me a call if he found a party or some small but notable gathering worth attending.

Anyway, Saturday finally rolled around, and since Mom was in the kitchen buried in work, getting the car for our little road trip wasn't hard.

I suppose you're probably wondering why I never borrow my dad's car. No point. He's been ridiculously overprotective since the "driveway incident," which is absurd because it really wasn't my fault. How was I supposed to know Mom was parked *outside* the garage door instead of inside like a normal person? And not only was she on the other side of the door, she was parked *directly behind* Dad's car, so when I opened the door and started to back out, well . . .

And it really wasn't *that* bad. Dad had a fit, though, and since then it's been next to impossible to pry the keys out of his hand.

Since Mom was preoccupied *and* facing away from the keys, I trotted down the stairs, sent an arm into the kitchen, and silently slipped the keys off the hook and into my pocket. I took a couple steps toward the garage, mumbled something about going out for a while, and bolted.

I'd talked to Michael on Friday afternoon, and he'd asked me to pick him up at Flap's. To be honest, I wasn't sure whether I'd see him or not. I figured he'd probably worked himself into a minor stroke thinking about the visit and decided to hide under his bed with a pocket Bible and his *Field Guide to Naked Old Men in Diapers*, but when I turned down Flap's street, there he was—on the stoop and reading a book, of course—but at least he was there.

When he saw me, he tucked the book into his backpack.

"Hi," he said, sliding in and closing the door.

"Flap wondering what you're up to?" I said.

"Yes."

"What'd you tell him?"

"Movies."

"Oooh, our first date, huh?"

He stared at me.

"So," I said, pulling into traffic, "what should we do on the ride up? Sing songs? Play Truth or Dare?"

"It's only about forty minutes, isn't it?"

"Yes, but it's a *road trip*, Michael," I said. "You have to get into the spirit of the thing."

He thought about this for a minute.

"I don't really know any songs," he said.

"You would if you'd been listening to classic rock as I instructed," I said, frowning.

I glanced over at him. He squirmed a bit.

Probably worried I'll force him to sing.

Well, if it upset him that much, maybe I would. Then again, there were other, more interesting ways to make him uncomfortable. I thought for a minute.

What do I want to know?

"So what's with the Bible study? You joining the priesthood?" I said.

"I've thought about it," he said quietly.

"And . . .? Is it the celibacy thing?"

"No."

"So it *is* the celibacy thing," I said, nodding.

"No, I'm not Catholic."

"What's the difference?"

"Priests are Catholic, and I don't believe in the tenets of the Catholic church." Before I could ask, he said, "I don't believe what they believe."

"Thanks for dumbing it down."

He looked to see if I was angry. I wasn't.

"I have thought about becoming a minister," he said.

"Is that like a super-priest?"

He looked out the window.

I sighed. "Michael, it's not a very long drive, but I would hate to have to make it unpleasant for you."

But he wouldn't come around. I squeezed the wheel hard with both hands and tried to keep my voice casual.

"I'd be a good priest," I said.

"You?" Michael said, a little too strongly.

"Yes, me. I think I know a little more about people than you do."

"And what does that mean?"

"It means I know how to handle them. So do priests. They're all just sheep-herders."

"Shepherds," he said.

"What's the difference?"

"Nothing, I guess."

"They're right about one thing—people are sheep," I said. "And it's our job to herd them around."

"Whose job?"

"Smart people. Like you and me," I said. "People want to be led, Michael. They want to be told what to do. It's easier than thinking."

"But that's not a minister's primary responsibility," he said. "Ministers are concerned with the spiritual well-being of their congregation."

"Minister? I'm going to be a priest," I said.

"You're Catholic?" Michael said, dubiously.

"Maybe."

My mom's Catholic. Every once in a while, she actually succeeds in dragging us to church—usually a guilt-ridden Christmas or a reluctant Easter visit. Church is like visiting an elderly relative. You know you're supposed to go more than twice a year, but never seem to find the time.

Our church had a long name I could never get right, and fairly graphic images of suffering on most of the walls.

"Anyway," I continued, "priests—*and ministers*—tell people what to do, don't they? They tell them what to do and how to do it. They let their sheep know if they've been bad or good—hey, kind of like Santa Claus! Then they tell people what they need to do to get their presents when they die. "Michael," I said, turning to face him, "I think I just figured out why God has a long white beard . . . Santa!"

Michael stared at me a second, then turned back to the window.

"What are you doing?"

"You're not being serious," he muttered.

"Oh, yes I am, Michael. Do you honestly believe the average sheep thinks about 'spiritual well-being' as much as you do?"

No response.

"Do you?"

"Probably not," he said.

"Of course not," I said. "And why do you think the average sheep goes to church?"

Michael shrugged.

"Do you think it's because they love rolling out of bed on Sunday so they can sit on uncomfortable benches and listen to someone tell them they're going to hell?"

Michael tried to interrupt, but I was on a roll.

"They go because they think they have to," I said. "They think if they show up and kneel when they're supposed to and move their lips during the songs, God's going to let them into heaven."

"I don't—"

"Oh," I said. "And they do it for their kids. They're too lazy to teach their kids anything, so they drag them to church and turn the kids into sheep, too."

I wanted to keep going but temporarily ran out of material. I hate it when I run out of material or lose my train of thought. It gives someone else a chance to jump in, and I'm only a good conversationalist when it's my turn to speak.

So I usually ask a question when I run out of material. Questions give you a chance to reload.

"So why don't you want to be a minister anymore?"

He answered, but not loud enough for me to hear.

"What?"

"I don't think my faith is strong enough," he repeated.

"So?"

"So?!" Michael said. "How can you be a minister if you don't . . . if you're not sure what you believe?"

"So you're telling me that all the ministers in the world believe every bit of what they're saying 100 percent of the time?"

He hesitated.

"Michael?"

"Yes, I think most of them—"

"Most of them?"

"*Some* of them probably have . . . I'm sure they have moments . . ."

"You don't sound very sure."

"So you think they're all liars?" he said, flushing.

"Maybe not all of them," I said, "but a good minister's probably like a good salesman."

Michael looked like I'd forced a lemon wedge into his mouth.

"Sure! You're a salesman and God's your product," I said. "There's a lot of competition, though. You've got your Jewish product, your Catholic product, and so on. And there's the imported stuff—Buddhism and so forth. Then you've got the cults at the very bottom. They're like the guys on the shopping channel—they've got to give you the hard sell because their product is such a piece of crap."

Michael was staring at me.

"Anyway, you've got your product, and you know it's pretty good, but you've got to dress it up a little. You need them to want your product more than they want the other ones."

Michael tried to interrupt again. I held up my hand. "I'm not talking about lying," I said. "You just don't mention the fine print right away. Let them think they're eligible for the gold card and throw in the details right when they're signing the contract: 'Oh, by the way, not everyone gets the bonus package. But if you want it, here's what you need to do.'"

I was pretty happy with myself when I finished, so I was a little annoyed when I glanced at Michael and found him staring out the window again.

"So?" I said.

"So?" he said, without turning.

"What do you think?"

"I think you missed the point."

"What the hell do you mean?" I said.

I was pretty pleased with the case I'd built and not real happy with the reception it had received.

"And quit talking to the window or I'm going to roll it down for the rest of the trip. I can do that, you know."

Actually, I wasn't sure if I could. There were a lot of buttons in Mom's car and I didn't know what half of them did.

I felt kind of bad when he turned to face me. He looked like he was going to cry. Or get sick. I didn't want to see him cry, and I definitely didn't want a spray of vomit in my direction.

"I couldn't do that," he said quietly.

"Do what?"

"Be a salesman."

"Why not?"

"Because it's not honest," he said.

"Why not?"

"Because I need to believe the things I say."

I sighed. "But you just said some of them have doubts," I said.

He shrugged. "I'm different, I guess."

I guess? I held my tongue and tried to hit him from a different angle: "So why did you want to be a salesman?"

"What?"

"A minister? Why did you want to be one?"

"I wanted to help people," he said.

"Michael, helping people is hard. *Telling* people what they need is the same thing, and it's much easier. That's how you need to think of it."

"It's not honest."

"Okay, so who do you want to help?" I asked.

"Huh?"

"Well, do you want to help poor people? Hungry people? Oh, wait—I guess if you're poor, you're also probably hungry, right? Do you want to help children? Old people?"

He didn't respond.

"Well?"

"I don't know," he said, flushing. "Everybody, I guess. Spiritually."

"Didn't Jesus already do that?"

He tried to look out the window.

"Michael, I'm being serious," I said. "Are you listening to yourself? What kind of goal is that—'I want to help everyone'?"

"What's wrong with it?" He was bright red now.

"You sound like a creepy Christmas card or some adorable figurine. 'I want to make the whole world happy!'"

"Let me out."

"What?"

"Stop the car. Let me out," he said.

"Michael," I said calmly, "remember when I said you weren't allowed to take every comment seriously? You've got to stop freaking out every time someone gives you a little shit."

"So what's next?" Michael said. "Are you going to start throwing me up against lockers too?"

That kind of put a damper on things. I hadn't meant to push so hard, but he was just so irritating sometimes. Time to change course and redirect the conversation—prop him up a bit. Luckily, something came to mind just when I needed it.

"Michael," I said, brightly, "you're just like Jesus."

No response.

"Didn't he get beat up all the time? And didn't people think he was weird?"

"Well, that's not quite—"

"They threw rocks at him, right? People throw rocks at you once in a while."

He scowled.

"Oh, hold on," I said, remembering something. "Maybe not."

He waited.

"Jesus probably didn't have that little problem you have."

Michael stared.

"The faith thing," I said. "I'm guessing he was pretty sure of himself."

"Not all the time. Not on the cross," said Michael.

"There," I said happily. "See? I'm right."

No response. I glanced over. He wasn't flushed anymore, and the scowl had dried up at the edges. I decided to give him a break. At this point, we were about fifteen minutes from Baltimore. It dawned on me that, in a little while, I might be shaking hands with Michael's father.

I couldn't really picture him, though. I kept seeing a slightly taller version of Michael with bags under his eyes, so I stopped trying. Instead, I thought about the bookstore Michael was all cramped-up about and wondered if we'd be able to find it.

"So where's your dad?" I asked.

Michael pulled the address out of his backpack.

I nodded. "What exit?"

"Martin Luther King, Jr. Boulevard. It's still pretty far."

"Okay."

I decided not to bother him for a bit. I figured both of us needed some time inside our heads.

We cruised along for a while, skimming through suburbia, then started to make our approach. The traffic got a little heavier, and suburbia got taller and thicker, and pretty soon we were curving down the ramp and spilling into the city.

"Take a right at the next light," Michael said from behind his directions.

I nodded. "How far away are we, anyway?"

"Five, maybe six miles," Michael said, studying the directions as if he weren't completely sure.

I think I told you we live pretty close to D.C. Driving through Baltimore wasn't all that different than driving in D.C. Of course, I wasn't familiar with any of the streets, but on the whole, no big deal.

I let Michael give me the occasional direction and tried to sightsee when I could.

We drove through a stretch of town that might have been the edge of a business district, then past a few blocks of restored row houses and into a little shopping area.

After the shopping area, though, things weren't as pretty.

I'm sure you've heard the expression "other side of the tracks." Well, I never did see any actual railroad tracks, but somewhere after the shopping area, it was like we'd crossed an invisible line. The change was like a long, low cloud sliding in front of the sun—the kind of shift you feel on the inside. Outside, it was still bright, but after we crossed "the line," things were different. The city became much more industrial. Rows of delivery and utility trucks parked along long, flat stretches of hard-packed dirt. Machine shops, marble and granite, paint. And lengths and lengths of tall chain-link fence.

Then, up a slight incline past billboard after billboard—mostly advertisements for gentleman's clubs, booze, and DUI lawyers.

"At least they're in the right order," I said to myself.

"What?" Michael asked, shaking his head and turning away from the window.

I gave a return head shake, letting him know it was nothing important.

Once we leveled off, the buildings become shorter and shabbier. Local businesses, signs written in languages other than English, and restaurants that looked like someone had thrown them together with a couple hundred bucks.

Street signs were missing and people weren't out walking like they had someplace to be. They were in little groups in front of convenience stores. Or slumped at bus stops like they'd been there for a day or two.

We stopped at a light and a group of kids crossed and gazed at us as they passed by. They were probably the same age as Michael, but seemed larger somehow. Older and more capable. We could hear their voices but not the words. One or two nodded at our car, then put a suggestion in the nearest ear. A few faces looked back at us with renewed interest, the same lazy half-smile in their eyes.

"How close are we now?" I asked.

"Pretty close," Michael said, uncertainly.

"Seen your bookstore yet?" I joked.

I tried to float down the road as quietly as possible.

Finally, we were close enough that we had to slow down and keep an eye on the numbers. I was a little surprised when I realized we weren't looking for a house. It was going to be one of the four- or five-story brick buildings that now grew along either side of the street.

Had I really been nervous walking around Michael's neighborhood? I couldn't imagine having to move up and down these streets every day.

"There it is," Michael said, pointing. He didn't sound thrilled.

I drifted over to the side of the road and rolled to a stop.

"Michael," I said, "I don't know how long I want to leave the car here."

He stared at the building and nodded.

We hurried across the street and hustled up the sidewalk toward the entryway. His father's building had dull, faded tan bricks. The balconies attached to the front looked like they were ready to come apart. The building itself looked like every other structure in the area, and they all looked like they wanted to be left alone so that they could sink into the ground.

I opened the front door, only to find another one a few feet in front of me. To the left was a list of names, each with a little black button beside it.

"What the hell?" I said.

"I think it's locked," Michael said, pulling on the second door. "I think we have to push the button and he'll let us in."

"Which one's his?"

Michael pointed to a last name. I pushed the button and we waited.

Nothing happened.

After a few awkward moments, I said, "Well, I guess—"

Suddenly, I heard an extremely loud buzzer. "What the hell?!" I yelled. The noise finally stopped when Michael reached around me and opened the second door.

"Oh," I said. Inside, it was dark and, of course, smelly.

"He's on the third floor," Michael said, heading up the stairs.

"How do you know?"

"His number starts with a three. That means he's on the third floor."

Michael seemed to be in charge now. I wasn't quite sure how I felt about that, although it did free me up to imagine what might be happening to the car.

We followed the staircase up. Each landing had a window that looked out over the street. I could just see the back of the car from each. So far, so good. The tires were still there, and the windows weren't broken.

There wasn't much light on the third floor, and the hallway was narrow. I imagined people coming out of their doors to get a good look at us, but no one did. Then, to make myself feel better, I imagined the same people walking their cats up and down the hallway, because that's what it smelled like: cat pee.

Music pumped through the walls from a couple apartments, and someone's loud voice from another. And then there were doors that were absolutely quiet. These doors were even more unsettling. I don't know how, but for some reason I knew there were people on the other side. People with one eye pressed to the peephole—following us, weighing possibilities.

Finally, we came to his father's door. There was music, but it wasn't loud.

We looked at each other.

"You want me to knock?" I said.

He looked as if he wanted to say yes but shook his head instead. I made some room, and Michael tapped on the door. His knuckles barely touched the wood.

"Michael," I said.

"Fine," he said, frowning, and raised his hand to knock again. But before he could, the door popped open and swung back a few inches to the end of its short chain.

A girl peered out at us.

I looked at Michael.

"Who are you?" the girl said.

At first, I thought she might be "the girlfriend" or something, but she looked pretty young. She might have been our age, but it was hard to tell. She could have been a year or two older, but just as easily could have been a little younger. Her eyes were dark and scooped-out underneath. She might have been pretty if she hadn't looked so tired. "I'm his—he's my father," Michael managed, flushing nicely. I made a mental note. We definitely needed to work on talking to girls. Michael looked like he was going to have a stroke.

She stared at him. "What?" she finally asked.

"Do you think we could come in?" I asked. "There's a lot of cat pee out here."

She just stared. I started to say something else, but before I could, she decided to unchain the door. She seemed to be operating on a kind of five-second delay, which made me wonder what she was on and why she was letting two strangers in.

There wasn't much in the living room—not much furniture, that is. To the left was a couch that was even worse than the one in Michael's house. Past the couch was an armchair that looked like someone had beaten it with a chain. On the floor in front of the couch, there was a TV and next to the TV, the stereo we'd heard from the hallway.

It reminded me of Michael's computer. It was new, very expensive, and completely out of place. Records grew in clumps around the stereo— not CDs, but vinyl records. There were long rows of records pushed up against the living room walls, stacks on the floor, and boxes of them scattered here and there. Somebody *really* liked music.

"You don't have any records, do you?" I asked the girl.

"What?" she asked, about five seconds later.

I pointed to the records and tried to smile.

"Oh," she said, sounding relieved.

"What do you listen to?" I asked.

"He listens to a lot of different stuff."

"So what do *you* listen to?" I asked again.

"I don't know. I like anything," she said, smiling.

I almost started a game with her—almost started to mess with her—but it was the smile that stopped me. It was a sad smile, as if she were apologizing. It's not much fun to mess with such an easy target, and I had a feeling that a lot of people had messed with her. It was probably why she wanted to be five seconds behind the world.

"So is he here?" I asked.

"He just got out of the shower."

We stood in the middle of the living room a while. She and I stared at each other while Michael looked at the records.

"So," I said, "do you think he'll . . .?" But she suddenly turned and left the room. Without following her, it was hard to tell where she'd gone. I looked at Michael.

"Maybe she went to get him," Michael said.

"Who the hell is that?" I said, pointing to the album he was holding. There was a goofy-looking guy with a beard on the cover holding a bright blue violin.

Michael stared at it, smiling.

Wow, I thought, *she and Michael have the same smile . . . If I didn't know any better . . .*

Something went off in my head, and I felt like I was waking up for the second time that day.

"Michael," I said, just as his father rounded the corner.

"Yeah?" his dad demanded. His belt wasn't buckled, and his hair was still wet. Michael definitely looked like Mom. Remember my theory? That everyone looks like one of six animals? Michael and Mom favored the rodent, but Michael's father fell into the horse category. The eyes, though—the eyes were the same.

Michael just stared.

"What'd you want?" his father said. Then, pointing to the girl, he said, "Did Chrissy let you in?"

I didn't know which question to answer, so I didn't say anything.

"Who are you?" he asked.

"I'm Matthew, and this is Michael."

"Okay," he said, obviously trying to calm himself. "One more time: What the hell are you doing in my apartment?"

I tossed him a grenade.

"Michael's your son."

Michael's father's face did some pretty bizarre things. At first, it looked as if the five-second delay was catching. Then his mouth tried to smile. However, his face wasn't in the mood, and he ended up looking constipated. Then his color ran away, and he looked as if he might fall to one side.

The girl was watching every change—her eyes were wide and her mouth hung open like a dead fish. She looked so ridiculous, I started to laugh. That got everyone's attention.

"Sorry," I said, "I'm not really laughing. Just nervous."

Michael's father turned back to Michael, but now the girl was staring at me and sporting a *really* goofy smile. She reminded me of some farm kid with overalls and big buck teeth.

This got me laughing harder, which, in turn, got her started.

"Sorry," I gasped.

Michael was frowning at me, and his father was frowning at the girl. I tried my hardest to pull it together, but just couldn't manage. She and I were feeding off each other.

"All right, that's enough, Chrissy," Michael's father said sternly.

She looked at him, then over at me, and we both ended up laughing even harder.

"Go to your room!" he said.

She stumbled down the hall, and I decided to head for the hallway.

"I'll be back," I said, although I don't know why. I'm sure at that point no one wanted me back, except maybe the girl.

Out in the hall, it took me a full minute to stop, and even when I did, I was still having little spasms of giggles here and there. I couldn't forget her face—both the dead-fish look and the farm-girl grin.

I tried to worry about being out in the hall by myself, but couldn't. Probably because I'd left the door open just a little, in case anyone came after me with an ice pick.

Eventually, I settled against the wall next to the door and listened.

"So, how'd you get here?" I heard his father ask.

"Matthew drove me," Michael said.

"He a friend of yours?"

"Yeah."

Well, it's about time.

There was an uncomfortable silence. It happened a lot during their conversation, so I'm not going to try and find different ways to describe it. When it happens, you'll just see the words, "Uncomfortable Silence."

"How'd you find me?" his father asked.

"Internet."

"Computers. Of course," his father grumbled.

Uncomfortable Silence.

"Is that your girlfriend?" Michael asked.

"Who, Chrissy? God, no. She's my daughter. She's . . ."

He stopped.

Uncomfortable Silence.

"Why'd you come up here?" his father asked.

"It was Matthew's idea," Michael said.

I decided to punch him when we were alone.

"He thought Mom might be lying," Michael continued.

"Lying? About what?"

"About you being . . . about you drinking a lot."

Uncomfortable Silence.

"I used to," his father said. "I've been trying to clean myself up a little."

There was a pause not long enough to qualify as an uncomfortable silence.

"It's been about two years now," his father said.

"That's good," Michael said.

"You don't drink, do you?" his father asked.

I almost started laughing again.

"Me? No—not at all," Michael said.

"That's good," his father said, seriously. "It's something you never want to get into. Our family can't handle it. Your grandfather was a drunk. I'm a drunk."

"But you stopped, right?" Michael asked.

"So? I'm still a drunk."

"You are?"

He nodded. "I could go back to it in a heartbeat. I want to at least once a day."

"What happens?"

"What do you mean?" his father said.

"When you're dr—when you're drinking. Is it that bad?"

Uncomfortable Silence.

"The first few drinks are okay," he said. "But after that, something just goes wrong inside my head."

Shorter Uncomfortable Silence.

"What does Chrissy . . .?" Michael asked in a small voice.

"She knows when to disappear."

Michael must have looked worried.

"I'm not saying I get violent. I don't hit my daughter," his father said firmly. "But I get to a place where I don't want anyone else around. And if there is someone around, I can get mean. Chrissy used to know when it was time to clear out and go to her room."

Pause.

"But that hasn't happened in years," he finished, quietly.

Uncomfortable Silence.

I was over my silliness now and wanted to see what was going on, but didn't feel like I could just stroll back in and watch, so I repositioned myself until I could just see both of them through the crack in the door.

I was surprised. Michael's father was bending down beside a stack of records. Michael was standing a few feet away, looking out a window. I guess I had imagined them facing each other.

"Mom said you left us," Michael told the window.

"She told me to sober up or leave," his father said. "And back then I couldn't let it go, so I had to leave."

It took Michael a while to get the next question out: "Didn't you want to see me?"

"Of course I did. A couple of times I got in the car to come down there."

Pause.

"I just couldn't do it, though. It seemed impossible," he said.

"Why?"

"Seeing the old house, knocking on the door, asking to see you. Then having to explain to my own son who I was . . ."

The last few words sounded weird, as if a bug had suddenly zipped into his throat.

"So you never came down?" said Michael.

"Look," his father said angrily, "I'm telling you the truth, okay? I'm not trying to make excuses. I've imagined this day a hundred times, and I told myself, as hard as it might be, I was going to be honest. And that's what I'm doing. I'm sorry if you don't like it."

"I didn't say—"

"Besides, I had Chrissy to worry about. She wouldn't stay with a babysitter when she was young, and I wasn't going to bring her with me to meet you."

His father slammed a record down and stood up. The atmosphere suddenly changed. There was a special feeling to this emerging quiet, like the doors we'd passed in the hall.

"Is something wrong with Chrissy?" Michael asked.

"Yeah . . . but they don't know what. The schools tried to tell me she was retarded, but that's not it. The doctors said that wasn't it."

I felt kind of bad about laughing at her now, but how was I supposed to know? I visualized her face—the goofy one—and almost started up again. I'm sorry, okay? I guess I'm just a bad person.

"Is she my sister?" Michael asked.

"Half-sister."

Pause.

"Look, I've got to get ready for work," said Michael's father. "You guys kind of surprised me."

I could see the disappointment on Michael's face from across the room.

"Why don't you come back again sometime when we can sit down and talk?" his father said.

Michael nodded.

His father disappeared around the corner. It was a good time for me to slip back in.

Michael turned to stare at me.

"How do you feel?" I asked.

But Michael, too, was suddenly caught up in the five-second delay.

"Michael?" I tried.

Eventually, he nodded. A door opened somewhere out of sight and we heard light footsteps. Chrissy wandered back into the living room and up to us.

"Where's Dad?" she asked.

"I think he went back there," I said, pointing.

She looked at me instead of following my finger.

"Are you leaving?" she asked.

"I think so," I said.

"Are you coming back?"

"I don't know. Maybe . . . Do you know who he is?" I asked, pointing at Michael.

He tried to smile.

"Are you my brother?" she asked.

"I think so," said Michael. "I mean, I'm your half-brother."

She stared. I counted: one, two, three, four.

"Half-*what*?"

"He's related," I clarified. "Cute, isn't he?"

She looked at me and laughed.

"Uh-oh, we'd better not start that again," I said, which made her laugh harder.

"Chrissy," her father said, coming down the hall, "don't start."

She put a hand over her mouth and tried to shove the laughter back in. Michael's father handed him a scrap of paper.

"Next time, give me a call first," he said. "I mean, you're always welcome, but call next time and we'll make some plans."

"You're going to work *now*?" I asked.

"I work better in the evenings and weekends . . . Keeps me out of trouble," he said.

"What do you do?" Michael asked.

"I'm a colorist," he said.

"A what?"

"I work on comic books—on the illustrations."

"You draw comic books?" I said.

"Not exactly. I work on the look. On the colors."

"You're a professional colorer?" I said.

"Kind of," he said, with a half-smile.

"Cool."

"Where'd you park?" he asked.

"Out in front," I said, hooking my thumb over my shoulder.

His eyebrows lifted. "Really? Hope it's still there."

It wasn't what I wanted to hear.

"Next time, park on one of the side streets," he said.

I started to pull Michael toward the door.

"So, I'll call you sometime," Michael said, holding the scrap of paper like it was a winning lottery ticket.

His father nodded.

"Thanks for having us," I said, dragging Michael away. "Nice meeting you. Bye-bye, Chrissy."

Chrissy stared for a few seconds, then started giggling.

"Well, goodbye," Michael said.

"You'll come see me again?" his father asked.

Michael nodded as I pulled him out the door. I kept him moving down the hall and toward the stairs. Looking out from the top-floor window, I could just see the back of the car.

Well, it's still there.

"Matthew . . ."

"Not now. Car first."

We hurried down the stairs, through the double doors, and out onto the sidewalk.

The car looked okay—all the wheels were there, and no windows broken.

Wait a minute.

"What the hell is that?" I said, darting across the street.

"What?"

"The windshield, Michael. What the . . .?"

I stopped. It was a huge glob of bird shit.

"Oh," I said.

"Wow, that's big," Michael said, impressed.

"Get in," I said, scowling.

I started the car and tried to run the windshield wipers. If you ever have a really big glob of bird shit on your windshield, don't just run the wipers through it. Big mess.

I used about a gallon of wiper fluid trying to make it disappear. Michael's side got nice and clean, but mine was one big smear. There were a couple breaks right around eye level, though, and that was enough for me. I took a quick look over my shoulder and whipped the car around.

A car horn blared and I almost soiled myself bracing for the impact, but we made it.

"Must have been a car," I said as we headed back toward the highway.

I glanced at Michael. He looked like he was a couple blocks away, still talking to his father. I let him stay there most of the way home. I didn't ask, but I had a feeling Michael wasn't interested in finding that Baltimore bookstore anymore.

CHAPTER 10

Before dropping Michael off at Flap's, I started to ask him if he'd officially moved in, but realized Michael might not be in the mood to hang out with Gut after seeing his real father.

Back at home and in my room, the phone rang. I looked at it, saw Jack's number, and silenced it. I guess I wasn't in the mood for company either. Jack didn't leave a message. He called me again later from a party and left a very un-nice message. It was typical Jack, and the main reason I enjoyed his company. The message said: "Hi. This message is for Matthew. Eat it."

I stayed put the rest of the night, watching TV in bed until I passed out.

Wanda called Sunday, but I didn't pick up. Guess I still needed some time to process things, which was kind of strange. Why the hell would *I* need to process anything? It wasn't *my* dad. And why did my thoughts keep drifting to Chrissy instead of Michael and his father?

That one bothered me more than a little, so I shoved it toward the back of my head and locked it in a little bathroom I constructed years ago for bothersome thoughts and memories just like it.

On Monday, I didn't go out of my way to find Michael. I figured he would want some time to overanalyze everything. Besides, if he really needed to find me, he would. So we passed each other in the halls Monday and Tuesday and nodded or smiled but didn't really talk much, which was fine.

For some reason, I couldn't stop Chrissy from popping up in my head. Even though I had relegated her to the back bathroom, somehow, she'd found a key and kept sneaking up on me. So instead of repeatedly hauling her back to the smelly bathroom, I started thinking about Michael again.

Despite the rumor I'd spread, Michael was still getting hassled a bit during the school day. Traditions are hard to break, I suppose, but it wasn't so much everybody picking on him now—just a few of the hardcore guys like Leonard. So while things weren't perfect, they had certainly improved.

On Wednesday, I did some Michael-work during Astronomy. Maybe he needed a new look. Or an exciting new hairdo.

And Gut. I needed to ask Michael if he'd initiated the Classic Rock Assault. Even if he hadn't, it was almost time to launch a new offensive. Gut was wobbly, but Michael's sudden interest in Aerosmith wouldn't be the crowbar that sent him over.

So what next?

When the bell rang, I shoved my stuff into my backpack and trudged out the door.

And that's when Wanda walked past.

She turned her head, gave me a haughty look, and kept going.

Wanda!

"I love you," I said, catching up with her.

"Uh-huh," she said with a sniff.

"I tried to call you last night," I lied.

"Please," she said, stopping at her locker.

"It's just been crazy lately," I said.

"Demanding having a new friend, isn't it?"

"You wouldn't believe," I said, sagging against an adjacent locker.

"Better be careful who you hang out with," she said. "I hear Michael beat up a bunch of gangstas outside the Crossbow?"

"He sure did," I said, smiling.

"Mm-hmm . . ."

"Hey, how'd the poker thing go?" I asked.

She smiled.

"That good, huh?"

"Maybe. What'd you want?" she asked.

"I got an acting job for you."

Wanda was big into drama. It was an interest that baffled me.

"What's the job?" she said, casually.

I smiled. "Michael's girlfriend."

She didn't answer. Instead, she resumed her rummaging. I was trying to think of *something* that might persuade her when she said, "Could be fun."

We were between classes, but I gave her as much background as I could (which wasn't a lot, considering the idea had just occurred to me).

"So what's he like?" she said.

"Smells a little musty sometimes, but not bad, really."

She narrowed her eyebrows. "Did I ask how he smelled?"

I tried again: "Nice—too nice, actually . . . Likes to look at old men in diapers . . . Doesn't listen very well."

"Sounds like you."

"I don't like old people," I said.

"How should I play it?" she wondered.

"You'll do it?"

"*If* I do it. How should I play it *if* I decide to do you a big favor."

I tried to stifle my excitement. "I don't know. What do you think?"

She bent forward to shove some books into her backpack.

"I could do Angry Black Girl."

"What's Angry—?"

She straightened and sent an impossibly long index finger toward my face.

"No you di'ant!" she yelled, head moving from side to side like a cobra. She held the pose a moment, winked, then let the finger drop.

"Nice!"

"Or Brooding Black Girl," she said. "Brooding Black Girl doesn't say much. She just looks really pissed off about everything."

"Sounds delightful."

"She's easy," Wanda said, throwing her backpack over one shoulder. "I use her when I'm tired. Hmm . . . maybe Super Smart Girl," she said, closing her locker.

"What's *she* like?"

"Talks a lot. Very into school. Does a lot of community projects and after-school activities."

I nodded.

Wanda started walking. I followed.

"And then there's Bad Girl. Bad Girl doesn't give a shit. Doesn't come to school much. Likes her drugs. Very slutty. Fun, but she can be a pain in the ass."

"What do you mean?"

"She's a little hard to control," Wanda said. "I never know what she's going to do, you know?"

I didn't but nodded anyway. We were headed toward the front of the school, and away from my next class, but if being late meant I got Wanda for the part, I'd take it.

"I've got a few others," she said, "but most are just variations on the four."

Confused, I tilted my head to one side.

"Sometimes it's good to mix a little of each," she explained. "Makes it more believable."

"For example?" I said.

"Well, there's a version of Super Smart Girl who's really slutty."

Like I said, Wanda was brilliant.

"When do you want to do it?" she asked.

"I don't know," I said. "Soon?"

"Can't do it Thursday."

"Okay, not Thursday. Friday, maybe?"

"Maybe."

"We'll probably need a car," I said.

Mom had been overly generous with her vehicle lately and I was expecting a correction at any moment.

She ignored the question, stopping outside the auditorium.

"Assembly?" I said, hopefully.

She shook her head.

"Oh, right," I said.

Drama.

"Coming to *Death*?" she asked, brightening.

"What?"

"*Death of a Salesman*," she said, tapping a poster on the wall.

"Oh, right. I was going to, but I think I have something that night."

"What night?"

"All of them."

Someone called her name. She looked into the auditorium but didn't respond.

"I might be able to help," she said, still looking over her shoulder. "Just not tomorrow."

"What's going on tomorrow?"

"Poker night."

"Why Thursday?" I said. "Why not play on the weekends?"

"Please," she said, turning back to me. "Weekend poker's for amateurs."

"You guys play for real money?" I asked, backing away toward my next class.

"Candy," she said.

I looked at her.

"How do you think I got a car, Beautiful?"

I stopped and watched her move toward the stage and into the darkness.

I was almost in love.

⸺⦿♪♪♪♪⸺

I caught Michael later that day. We were between classes. I was walking toward his locker and he was digging for something.

He was less than enthusiastic when I told him about Wanda.

"Wanda?" was all he could manage.

I closed my eyes and sighed. "Yes, Wanda. She's perfect."

"Am I going to . . . I mean, are we—"

"Are you going to have to touch her?" I asked. "Yes, Michael, you're going to have to touch her. You're going to have to touch a girl. It's got to be believable, just like the racing stuff."

"I've made out with girls before," Michael said, not bothering to look at me.

The phrase "made out" sounded ridiculous coming out of his mouth.

"When?" I asked.

He mumbled something.

"When?!"

"Fifth grade," he said quietly.

"What do you mean? Was it some kind of orgy?"

"What?!"

"Well, you just said you 'made out with girls' in fifth grade."

"Not at the same time."

"Uh-huh. Any women since your fifth-grade days?"

"Not really," he mumbled.

"Not really?"

"None, okay?"

"Don't get all cramped-up, Michael. I'm like a doctor," I said. "I need to know these things in order to treat you."

He stared at the floor, clenched his teeth, and nodded grimly.

"Now, when was the last time you had a good bowel movement?"

"What?"

"Kidding," I said. "Look, someone has to ask the hard questions. I can't have you turning bright red and giggling when Wanda grabs your hand."

"I'm not going to giggle," he snapped.

I thought for a moment. "You want to practice?" I said.

"What?"

"Should we practice holding hands?"

"No!"

"Fine," I replied. "But if you mess it up, I'm *really* gonna be pissed."

"I'm not going to mess it up."

"We're going to try Friday," I said. "And before you say, 'This Friday?!,' yes, this Friday."

He nodded.

"Oh, wait . . . Will Gut be there after school?"

"He's between jobs," Michael said, sourly.

"What about Mom?"

He shook his head.

"Too bad," I said. "But it'll have to do. We'll meet you in the parking lot after school, okay?"

Michael nodded. I left him standing by his locker.

Looking back, I can't understand why I didn't insist on a dress rehearsal. I don't know what I was thinking, letting Michael get away without one. I do remember hoping Gut would be mad enough to throw us all out of the house. Then again, I kept hoping he'd wear one of those sleeveless t-shirts, too.

I never get what I want.

CHAPTER 11

Watch a lot of gangster movies? If you do, then you've seen this shot about a hundred times: a group of made guys on their way to whack someone, walking toward the camera in slow motion. Drop a hard-ass song in the background and you've completed your gangster-film cliché.

Walking out to Wanda's car after the last bell felt just like that—for two of us, anyway.

Unfortunately, Michael looked like he was going to a funeral. He crawled into the backseat and tried sinking into the upholstery.

Oh, no you don't, I thought as I slid into the passenger seat.

"How you feeling, Wanda?" I asked.

She gave me a smile.

"Super Smart Girl?" I guessed.

She shook her head. "Don't know yet. We'll see. They usually decide for me."

"What?"

"The girls usually decide," she said. "I probably won't know until we're inside the house."

I nodded and tried to look like it made sense.

"Michael was in a fifth-grade orgy," I said as we pulled out of the parking lot.

"No I wasn't!" he shouted from the back.

"Wow. What school did you go to?" Wanda asked.

"One of those montagory schools," I said.

"*Montessori?*" she said, smiling.

"Whatever."

"What else is he into?" she asked.

"Heroin."

"Really?"

"He's lying," Michael said.

"What are you into, honey?" Wanda asked, glancing at Michael in the rear-view mirror.

I sighed when I didn't hear anything from Michael, guessing I'd have to keep prodding.

"Books, I guess," he muttered.

"Oh yeah? What kind?" Wanda asked.

"All kinds."

"Jesus," I said, shaking my head.

But for some reason, it didn't bother Wanda. "Got a favorite?" she asked.

"Book?" Michael asked.

"No, Michael—drugs. She's wondering if your favorite is heroin or opium."

"That's not what I—do you mean favorite book or favorite author?" he said.

"Either one," Wanda said. "How about both?"

And that's all it took. Michael was off and running.

"Well, I guess if I had to pick a favorite book . . . favorite *fiction* book . . . If I had to pick a favorite novel, I guess it would either be *Hitchhiker's Guide* or *I Heard the Owl Call My Name*."

"Oh yeah?" Wanda said. "How about favorite author?"

"Probably Hope Mirrlees."

I had to admit, I was somewhat impressed. Michael was talking to a real-live girl.

And not just any girl. Michael was talking to Wanda. But then again, we were in a car, and she couldn't yawn and wander off. I checked to see if Wanda was getting drowsy. Instead, I saw a strange little smile I'd never seen before.

"Hmm . . . didn't really like *Lud-in-the-Mist*," she said. "The writing's a little too flowery. But that's just me."

What is she talking about? Is she actually listening?

No response from the backseat. I glanced at Michael. He looked as if someone had just punched him in the stomach. His eyes were wide and his face was beet-red. His head looked dangerously close to some kind of explosion.

"You've read it?" he asked.

"Yep."

"How could you not like the language? It's incredible."

"Too much for me. I like my books a little tighter."

"Like what?" Michael said.

"Well—"

"And please don't say Ernest Hemingway," he said.

"Hell, no—give me a little credit, honey."

Michael and Wanda had a nice little book club chat after that, one that didn't involve or interest me. Thankfully, it was a quick ride.

"It's that one on the right," Michael said, leaning forward into the space between our seats.

Wanda rolled to a stop just before the start of his driveway. We sat in the car for a minute, staring at the tired little house.

I looked at Wanda, wondering what she was thinking. As usual, her face was impenetrable.

"You going to be able to do this, Michael?" I asked, turning.

Michael nodded. He looked okay now. Only his cheeks were flushed.

"You ready, Wanda?" I asked.

She didn't say anything. She was looking through me, toward the house.

"Wanda?" I tried again.

"Getting into character," she said quietly.

"Sorry."

Michael and I waited for our cue. Michael rummaged through his backpack, looking for something. He pulled out a thick paperback that had definitely seen better days—in fact, it looked like someone had played a few games of street hockey with it.

He glanced at Wanda, looking like something had suddenly occurred to him, but then sank back on his seat and started to read.

Without thinking, I opened the glove compartment and began to explore. Then I realized what I was doing and quickly shut the little door. Wanda didn't seem to notice, though.

I sat still for about ten seconds before I started to fidget. After a while, I bent forward to retrieve a scrap of paper peeking out from underneath my seat. When I came back up, Wanda was stepping out of the car.

I turned back toward Michael, but he was halfway out.

"Thanks, guys," I said to myself, hastily rolling out of the car after them.

Somehow, Wanda knew to use Michael's side door. Michael trailed behind her like a little kid trying to keep up with an angry parent.

Wanda came to a halt a step or two shy of the door. Michael hurried around her and began fumbling with the storm door, desperate to open it for her. He froze when she reached over and pushed her fingers through his hair.

"You ready, baby?" she said, her voice low.

He nodded, apparently hypnotized, and tried the door again. This time he managed to wrestle it free. He let Wanda through, then almost knocked me over making sure he was only a few inches behind.

"Nice," I said, but I didn't have an opportunity to complain in full. I wanted to make sure I saw Gut's face when he caught sight of Wanda.

As usual, the TV was on and Gut was in front of it. Wanda didn't waste any time. She strode right into the living room and stood in front of the TV as if she were going to start whaling on him. *Bad idea*, I thought— like getting between a mother bear and her cub.

"Excuse me," she said. "Can we sit down?"

Wanda towered over Gut. The back of his head was tilted up toward the ceiling. It was as if an athlete had suddenly hopped out of the TV.

"What's that . . .?"

Gut looked around, probably hoping to unravel the mystery of the unfamiliar girl. He relaxed a bit when he saw Michael sliding in at the other end of the couch.

"Have a seat," Gut muttered, shifting his fat ass in the opposite direction.

Unfortunately, I didn't have a good view of the initial reaction, but I did get the opportunity to watch Gut clumsily rearranging the cushions and trying to sweep a collection of crumbs and magazines onto the floor.

There was an elderly armchair to one side of the couch, down at Gut's end. I sat down gingerly, expecting it to give way. Wanda sat between

Michael and stepfather. She stared straight ahead, as if interested in the show, but sent a spidery arm across Michael's bony shoulders. The hand at the end of the arm toyed with his hair.

Gut wasn't quite so interested in his program anymore.

"Wobble, wobble," I said, smiling.

"What's that?" he asked.

"What's coming up?" I said, pointing to the TV.

But he was distracted again, this time by Michael's hand on Wanda's thigh. That one caught me by surprise, too.

"I don't know," Gut finally managed.

"You want something to drink, baby?" Wanda asked Michael.

Michael shook his head no, eyes never leaving the TV.

"How 'bout a sandwich? You want me to make you a sandwich?"

He shook his head again.

"Come on, baby. You got to be hungry after what we . . ." Wanda broke off and gave Gut a demure smile. He tried to return it, but his brain was finishing her sentence. He ended up looking like someone asked to smile for a snapshot after unwrapping a gift of leather mandals.

Eventually, he remembered that he should probably say *something*. He tried to clear his throat, but a weird gurgling noise came out. He got what he wanted, though. Everyone looked over at him.

"Don't think I've met you before," he mumbled.

"Wanda, handsome. Who are you?"

"Wendal," said Gut.

Wendal?!

"Michael's stepfather," he said.

Michael leaned over and whispered something in Wanda's ear.

"You behave," she said, giggling.

Gut was too stunned to respond and, honestly, so was I.

"So . . . you two going out?" Gut asked.

"Uh-huh," Wanda said. She cupped Michael's cheek and pulled his face toward her. "We are, aren't we, baby?" she said.

Michael pulled away, scowling.

"What's wrong?" she asked.

Wanda looked surprised. She was good. I couldn't tell if it was real or part of the act.

"Why do you have to say that all the time?" Michael asked.

"What do you mean?"

"Why do you always have to announce it like we're engaged or something?"

Wanda paused.

"Well, what do you *want* me to say?" she asked, smiling at Gut.

Instead of answering, Michael got up and headed for the kitchen. Wanda watched him go, considering.

In a moment, she began to smoothe her clothes. She made a show of plucking several hairs from her shirt and releasing them to the floor. Finally, she stood, stared at the TV a second, and headed into the kitchen.

As soon as she was around the corner, Gut and I looked at each other. We were both pretty relieved, although I should have been faking it.

"You'll have to get used to that," I said, jerking my head toward the kitchen.

"Why?"

"They're like that all the time."

Gut was having trouble processing this information. From the kitchen, I could hear Wanda's voice, low and rapid. Every so often, I'd hear Michael's, short and tense.

I noticed a car commercial and had a thought.

"Hey, that reminds me," I said, nodding at the screen. "I finally heard that story I was telling you about. Remember? The weird racing one?"

"Yeah?" Gut said, frowning.

"Yeah. It was about some guy named Ricky Earl. You know who he is?"

Gut nodded, glancing toward the kitchen again. Wanda's voice was a little louder.

"Turns out he's gay. Can you believe it?"

"It's just a rumor," Gut said, trying to fish a cigarette out of a half-empty pack.

"You sure? They pretty much said he was. Something about a nightclub at, like, two in the morning."

"Just 'cause he was in a gay club don't mean he's gay," Gut said around his cigarette.

Wow! He really has *thought about it!*

"Yeah, well, it doesn't exactly make you straight, either," I said.

"What do you mean?"

"Maybe he's confused."

Something shattered in the kitchen.

"Why don't you listen?!" Michael yelled.

We jumped up and hurried in.

Michael stood on one side of the tiny room. On the other, Wanda leaned against the sink. She looked worried. Something was dripping down the window above the sink, and there were pieces of glass all over the counter.

"Why do you get so mad?" she asked quietly.

"Because you never listen!"

"I just want to know where you're going tonight."

"No, you don't! You want to know who I'm going to see!"

"So? I got a right, don't I?" Wanda asked, looking at Gut.

Gut made some motion with his hands and lifted his shoulders. He threw in a headshake for good measure, as if hoping one of the three would be good enough.

"I already got a mother," Michael said.

"You'd best not be comparing me with your mother," Wanda said, sounding dangerous.

"Don't be stupid."

"Who you calling 'stupid,' little man?" Wanda said, pushing off from the counter and bumping up against him. Michael lifted his chin and met her eyes.

"You need to back off," he said.

"All right now," Gut said, taking a step forward and pitching his cigarette into the sink. Cautiously, he extended a hand between the two without actually touching anyone. I wondered who that hand was going to stop if things suddenly got ugly. "I think you two need a little break from each other."

Neither one moved. Their eyes were locked and glaring.

"Someone best get going before I decide the police should figure this out," Gut said.

Slowly, reluctantly, Michael tore himself away. "Don't call me!" he called over his shoulder, knocking the storm door open in front of him.

Wanda snatched a glass from the counter and hurled it at Michael's back. It shattered against the storm door as he left, showering the floor with more broken glass.

She stood for a moment, breathing hard, and jumped for the door.

"Don't you go chasing him now . . ." Gut tried, but the door was already shaking itself back into place. He looked over at me.

"Well, that wasn't too bad," I said.

"Wasn't too good, either," Gut said.

I shook my head. "Nah, I've seen much worse. I wish they'd figure out they're bad for each other."

Gut was staring at the door. The plastic window now had a nice crack running through it.

"I mean, I'm friends with both of them, but Michael needs to cut her loose," I said. "He just likes to know he can always get her back if he feels like it."

Gut kept staring, like he was waiting for one of them to come back in.

"Anyway, he's seeing somebody else."

"Why the hell does Michael have two girlfriends?" Gut said angrily.

"Because he can."

Gut shook his head and produced a broom and dustpan from one side of the refrigerator.

"That's what you get, though," I said, watching him sweep.

"Yep."

"Going out with someone like Wanda, you know?"

"Uh-huh."

He wasn't taking the bait.

"Black girls are like that, you know?" I said. "You don't want to mess with them."

"That don't matter," he said, without looking up. "People's people. She's just bad news."

I felt ridiculous.

I bent down and held the dustpan for Gut while he swept Wanda's glass off the floor.

"Thanks," he muttered.

"You going to tell him not to see her?" I asked.

"Won't matter. He don't listen to me," said Gut.

"Why not?"

"Lotsa reasons. I'm not his dad. He's a teenager. Can't do much with teenagers. You just got to ride it out."

"So why do you hate him?" I asked.

"I don't hate him," he said. "We're just different. I can't say nothin' around him or he gets all huffy and stomps off to his room. Got two boys from my first marriage. We joke around all the time. I give it to them, and they give it right back. I always figured it would help 'im—learnin' how to take a joke and learnin' how to give it back."

"Michael's different, though," I said. "He's not . . . he's not that way."

"Yeah, well, where the hell has that kid been lately?" Gut asked, standing. "Girls I never seen before. Girls he don't belong with. Throwing shit at each other. That ain't Michael. That ain't right."

"What do you mean?"

"Somethin's happened up there," he said, tapping his head with a finger. "I ain't surprised, the way he's wound so tight, but I ain't never seen him like that."

Gut stared at the cracked window. I stood up and dumped the glass into the trashcan.

"Me neither," I said.

"His mom worries like nobody you've ever seen," said Gut. "'Bout everything. Just about drives me crazy."

I didn't quite know what to do with this information. Should I agree? Disagree? Laugh?

"Thinks Michael's going to turn out like his father," he said, still staring out the door.

"Really?"

"Yep. Been tellin' her for years how ridiculous that is. Just look at him, for Christ's sake! Quiet as hell, readin' all the time, too shy for girls. On that computer every second he don't have a book in his face. You don't have to worry 'bout him hangin' out with his buddies and gettin' drunk."

Once again, I didn't know what to say, so I took my time putting the dustpan back into place.

"Maybe she was right," Gut told the door.

"How so?" I asked. A bad little feeling started squirming around in my stomach.

But Gut just shook his head. Turning, he said, "You need a ride home or somethin'?"

"Oh . . . no, thanks. Wanda drove."

"Yeah, well, she ain't here anymore."

I joined him at the door. Wanda's car was gone.

"Well, I'm not that far," I said, suddenly wanting to be outside. I just couldn't imagine sitting in a car with Gut. "Thanks, though."

"Yep," he said, tossing the broom back in place. I watched him grab a phone from the kitchen counter.

"You want me to tell Michael anything?" I said. "If I see him, I mean?"

Gut shook his head without looking over. I watched him dial, then wait for someone to pick up. I wanted to know who was at the other end of the line, but he just looked at me, so I had to smile and shove myself out the door.

I stood beside the stairs, up against the side of the house for a few seconds, but could only hear his voice, not the words. Time to start walking.

I had more than enough to keep me occupied.

At first, I thought I might find Wanda's car up ahead, or around the next curve. I thought maybe they'd driven off for effect. But I gave that up as I got farther down the road. Something told me I wasn't going to find them.

Nothing had gone the way I thought it would. Not one thing. Wanda's character was weird and annoying, Gut hadn't reacted the way he should have, and Michael—where did *that* come from?

And that's what worried me the most: Where *did* it come from? It could have been something he borrowed from TV, but how come it was so easy for him to slip into character? It had looked as natural as a reflex, and almost nothing Michael did looked natural. His body language, his voice, his conversation—usually Michael was either abrupt and overly loud, or nervous and unintelligible. So how come it was so easy for him to slip into character and lose everything that made him Michael? Did he want out of himself that badly?

And Gut? Our performance was supposed to knock him spinning, but here he was, actually *concerned* about Michael. And calling someone!

On the other hand, I'd accomplished what I'd set out to do.

Gut didn't think Michael was such a geek anymore. Now he thought

Michael was crazy.

I wondered what would happen. Would there be some kind of intervention? Would Michael come home to find a team of doctors sitting politely on the couch, sharing a cigarette with Gut?

I'd known a few kids who'd "gone away" for a while when they started to enjoy their drugs a little too much. Actually, Jack had taken a little "vacation" last year. He likes to "travel"—the "mental" kind, not the physical.

About a year ago, he started taking a few too many trips. I remember a party right before he left. It was warm, and everyone was outside, either in the backyard or crowded onto the deck. Jack got there before I did. It didn't take long to find him. He was on the deck in the middle of the crowd. Not standing and socializing, mind you. Jack wouldn't do that even on a good day. On this particular evening, he was lying flat on his back. In fact, he had arranged himself like Jesus on the cross and was just staring up at the sky, watching the clouds turn into rainbow sherbet.

It was an interesting situation, considering how many people were actually there. Most took a quick glance, realized it was Jack, and went about their business.

For some reason, I kept thinking about Jack as I made my way back to school. It's odd—Jack is almost subdued during an "adventure." Subdued for Jack, I mean. So even though the content is the same, the volume's a little lower. Can't remember if I mentioned Jack's affinity for the shock value method of interacting with both strangers and friends, but the "Jack Way" is sometimes more pronounced on a trip. Jack's filter is patchy at the best of times, and during his excursions, he kicks a gaping hole through it.

For example: Sometime after Jack's lie-down on the deck, we were in the backyard, wandering a bit, talking with different people.

Then, just as we were passing this huge guy we'd never seen before, Jack walks over to the guy, points up at his face, and yells, "Fudgepork!"

Everything within a ten-yard radius came to screeching halt.

"What?" the Big Guy demanded.

"Fudgepork," Jack clarified, then continued: "Hey, got a joke for you. What do you call a four-haired dick with shit growing on its knees?"

"What?"

"Jack," I tried, tugging on his arm.

"Come on, man," Jack said, clapping his hands. "What do you call a four-haired dick with shit growing on its knees?"

"What?" B.G. asked, cautiously.

"I have no idea," Jack said, laughing uncontrollably.

There was a pause as the words sunk in.

Fortunately, Big Guy started laughing too, and he and Jack became party friends.

Jack is what I would call naturally lucky. In situations like that one, the potential for things to get very ugly is always quite real and dangerously close. As it turned out, however, Jack's unconventional introduction to his newest friend helped me immensely. I'd seen his show a few too many times and was getting bored, so I pawned Jack off on B.G. for the remainder of the party.

Michael, though . . . Michael was nothing like Jack. Michael seemed naturally unlucky, and not the kind to skip seamlessly in and out of dangerous situations without a scratch.

And even though Jack was crazy lucky for a very long time, his luck eventually ran out, and he was sent on his very real vacation to sober up. If I remember correctly, it lasted about three weeks.

But how long is your vacation when the adults making the decisions think you're crazy?

The whole thing really started to bother me, so I tried to think of other, non-Michael things, like: Wasn't it about time Mom bought me my own car so I didn't end up in situations like this?

But of course, this just brought me back to the reason I was walking down the street in the first place. I sighed and shook my head.

I made it back to school and pulled out my phone. Then I realized Mom probably wasn't home yet and Dad was never back until just before dinner (on those evenings when he actually did show up).

I decided to walk around the building to the parking lot, hoping I'd run into someone I knew. At this point, even an acquaintance would do.

And just as I was turning the corner, a car came to a sudden stop right next to me.

"Matthew!"

"Hey, Nathan," I said.

Wonderful.

"Where you going?" he asked.

"Straight to hell."

He liked that one. "Need a ride?" he asked.

I hesitated, glancing at the half-full parking lot. Still a good number of cars, but not one that looked immediately familiar (at least from this distance).

"Yeah, sure," I said, getting in.

"What's going on with you?" Nathan asked, once we were moving.

"Not much."

"Coming to my party this weekend?" he asked.

"Probably," I said. It was the first I'd heard of it and the last place I'd think about going.

"Right on," he said. Then: "Hey! You hear about Michael?"

"Michael who?" I asked, sourly.

Nathan proceeded to recount Michael's epic visit to the Crossbow.

"Some dudes were giving Michael shit at the bar, but this one chick was hitting on me *hard*, and I didn't want to bail, even though I knew something was about to go down. So I moved her down to the other end. Ended up getting the best seat in the house *and* looking like a gentleman. You know what I'm saying?"

And even though I wanted the story to be over, I couldn't help myself. "Wait. I thought the fight happened *outside* the Crossbow?"

That only tripped him up for a second.

"Well, shit yeah—it *ended up* outside, but it started at the bar. And I was *right there*. Know what I'm saying?"

I did.

"So I just figured Michael would walk off or something, but . . ."

Nathan continued with the story, but I wasn't done yet.

"He come with you?" I asked.

"Huh?"

"Michael—he come with you? You guys hanging out now?"

"Michael?! Come on now."

He started to protest. It wasn't a pleasant choice, but I opted for the story instead of the denial.

"So it started off inside?" I asked.

"Yeah, it did. I figured he'd just walk off or something, but out of nowhere, Michael *slammed* this guy upside the face with a beer bottle!"

"No way," I mumbled, looking out the window.

"Hell yeah! I was right there, man! Anyway, the bouncers came over and tried to break it up, but Michael . . ."

It wasn't a long ride home, but it *was* a long ride home. Know what I'm saying?

CHAPTER 12

My phone buzzed around seven that evening. I was in my room. "The Michael and Wanda Show" at Gut's Laugh Factory had made it a tough day, and I just wanted to get into bed, but I wasn't comfortable giving myself a second-grader's bedtime, so I was glad for the distraction—even coming from the person on the other end of the line.

"Matthew?"

"Maybe."

"It's Michael."

I was quiet for a second. I was almost happy to hear from him. The whole performance with Wanda had thrown me, and it was a relief to hear old, awkward Michael again.

"What do you want?" I said.

"What are you doing?" he asked.

"Huh?"

"I mean," he stumbled, "are you going to do something tonight? Are you doing anything right now?

"Yes. I'm fondling myself, Michael."

"Oh . . . sorry. I didn't mean . . ."

"Something I can do for you?" I asked.

"Well, kind of . . . I mean, when you're done with . . . you know . . ."

"Michael?"

"Yes?"

"I'm not really fondling myself. And even if I was, why would I share that with you?"

"I don't know," he said. "I just need a ride."

"What do you mean?" I asked, becoming a bit more interested.

"Do you think—if you're not doing anything—do you think you could give me a ride?"

"Where?"

"To my father's."

I paused. Definitely not what I was expecting.

"Now?"

"Yes."

"Why?"

His turn to pause.

"It's kind of hard to explain," he said nervously. "I just want to get out of the house for a while."

"Why?"

"Can you just pick me up?"

"Sure," I said. "Then maybe I'll leave you somewhere. Kind of like me this afternoon? Remember?"

"I'm really sorry about that. I can explain. Can you just give me a ride?"

"Let me think about it."

"Okay," he said, nervously.

I thought about it. I'd been tired before the call, but I was awake now. Mom was home and in for the night. And he sounded desperate.

"Umm . . . ?" he said.

"Yes?"

"Should I call you back or something?"

"Huh?"

"So you can decide."

"You at home?" I asked.

"Jimmy's store."

"Of course. Do I have to talk to him?" I asked.

"No. He's not here."

"Where is he?" I said.

Michael hesitated, then said, "He's at my house."

I was suddenly *very* interested.

"What's he doing there?"

"Matthew."

"Is Gut there, too?"

"Yes."

"You're kidding."

"Matthew, *please*," he said, like a little kid about to have an accident. "Just come get me."

"Fine. I'll be there in a bit," I said.

"Thank you," he said.

"Actually, I don't know how long it'll take me. I've got to get the car from my—"

But Michael had hung up. I stared at the phone a moment, then tossed it gently on my bed.

Flap and Gut together at last?

Had they ever met? Flap was the kind of guy who'd have an "I Brake for Hobbits and Unicorns" bumper sticker on his car. Gut was the kind of guy who'd have that stupid little kid urinating on hobbits and unicorns in the back window of his truck.

But then again, Gut had a name now, and a life away from his couch. He wasn't a bigot, and he didn't hate his stepson. Making fun of him now wasn't much fun.

I still had Flap, though.

I went down the stairs, hit the landing, and turned into the kitchen. I found Mom in her usual spot.

"Do you live in the kitchen now?" I asked.

"Hilarious," she said, without looking up.

"Going out," I announced.

"Okay."

This was so startling I stopped in my tracks, hand dangling in mid-air on its way to the keys. Mom continued to frown over her papers until something told her I was still in the kitchen.

"So you're going out? Where are—where do you think you're going?" she tried, apparently realizing her mistake.

"Out," I said, quietly.

"Where?"

I didn't answer. Instead, I raised my eyebrows and nodded at the glass of wine next to her. "Something wrong?" I asked.

"No," she snapped. "It's just been a hard week, Matthew. That's all."

"Has it?" I asked.

"Yes, Matthew, it has."

She reached for the glass and took a sip.

Mom is absolutely not a drinker. More than one or two glasses and chances are good she'll barrel into a wall on her way to bed.

"I can have a glass of wine once in a while," she said, trying to sound casual.

"I'm concerned about your drinking, Mom. I'm a concerned family member."

She took another, larger sip.

In Mom's world, there were only a few occasions that called for a drink (two glass maximum)—weddings, funerals, and, sometimes, my father. Dad's not what you'd call an ideal husband.

"Dad?" I asked, nodded sympathetically.

"Be quiet, Matthew," she said. "Weren't you going somewhere?"

"Grandma finally die?" I said.

"Matthew!"

"These erratic mood swings are stunting my emotional development," I said.

"What development?" She smirked.

Now I was torn.

Michael had probably wet himself twice wondering when I'd get there. But on the other hand, Mother was feeling a bit scrappy this evening. It was such a rarity, I had to linger.

"I think it's time the three of us had a family meeting about your boozing," I said.

"Just go, Matthew," she said, waving me out of the kitchen.

"No," I replied, holding up a palm. "No, I will not turn my back on you. Not when you need me the most."

Mom groaned. I took out my phone and began pushing buttons. She looked up.

"Matthew? What are you—?"

"I'm sure I have his number in here somewhere," I said, scrolling through my contacts.

"*Don't* call your father! That's about the last thing I need right now."

"Ah, there he is," I said. "Do you want to talk to him or would you like me to explain?"

"Tell him to pick up some milk on his way home—if there's a store open at that hour."

Mom pulled a set of papers closer and began to read. I kept the phone close to my ear, but let it drop, deciding against holding a pretend conversation with Dad.

"What are those?" I asked, taking a step forward.

Something about the set of papers directly in front of her had caught my eye. I'm not sure if it was a name, the look, or what. But something about them was unusual.

Her reaction confirmed it. Before I could take a second step, she grabbed the papers and stuffed them under a nearby pile.

I wanted a look at those papers, but knew I wasn't going to get one if I pressed. And although it was quite unusual for me to do so, I reversed my original position and opted for that fake phone call with Dad after all. Pretending to hear something, I looked at the phone, then brought it quickly to my ear.

"Hello? Dad? Oh, thank goodness."

"Matthew," Mom warned.

"No, no . . . I'm okay. It's Mom . . . Yes, she's at it again."

"Give me that phone," she said.

I shook my head.

"Angry," I told the phone, "and abusive."

Mom narrowed her eyes. Then she smiled.

"Tell him about the milk," she said.

One more sip of wine and she was back to work.

Damn. Wonder what blew it? Oh well.

Making sure I remembered which pile those papers were in, I backed away from the table. After two glasses, maybe she'd forget this whole conversation.

"Okay then, I guess you're safe to leave alone. I'll be back at the usual time. Midnight?"

"I don't think so," she said.

I lifted the keys off the hook.

"What's that?" I asked.

"I want you back by—"

Unfortunately, the door to the garage swung closed before I could catch the rest of her sentence.

"Someone should really fix those doors," I said, heading for the car.

Although I expected to see an angry lady at any moment, the door remained in place as I started the car and pulled out of the driveway. Still hopeful, I didn't close the garage door until I was on my way up our street.

Oh, well—another day.

All things considered, the evening was picking up nicely. Something was going down at Michael's house and I had scored another win at home.

And the papers, I reminded myself. *Don't forget the papers.*

CHAPTER 13

It wasn't a long drive, but I couldn't stop thinking about Michael's phone call. What the hell was Flap doing at Michael's? It was a little late for a friendly game of *Magic*, and Michael's books were all well organized.

The possibilities were a little too overwhelming, and after a few minutes, I stopped guessing and turned up the radio. For all I knew, a massive house party was underway, and Michael was uncomfortable and wanted to leave. An image suddenly came to me: Flap and Gut grinding in the middle of the living room with Wanda pinned between them.

I almost had to pull over. The vision was that disturbing.

Eventually, I rolled to a stop near the Hole in the Wall sign. Michael was huddled on the stairs, reading.

"Good to see you again," I said, as he slipped in the front. "Did you guys have a good time? Wanda pregnant?"

"What?!" Michael said, freezing as he reached back for his seatbelt.

"Because sex with Wanda is about the only reason I'll accept for being stranded with Gut."

"Oh," Michael said. Maintaining eye contact, he slowly strapped himself in, as if afraid I might suddenly kick him out the door the moment he got close to buckling.

Good. Let him think it's a possibility. Who knows? I just might.

"I'm really sorry about that," he said.

It wasn't great, but it was something.

I watched him latch his belt, kept my eyes in Aggressive Mode a moment more, then pulled away from the curb.

"So you want to go to your father's?" I asked, bulling my way onto Route 30 and pointing us toward the highway.

He didn't answer.

"Okay . . . so why is Flap at your house?"

No answer.

"House party?" I asked, nervously.

Silence.

Car horns blared as I jerked the car to the side of the road.

"What are you doing?!" he yelled, grabbing the dashboard.

"I'm not your fucking chauffeur!" I snapped. "Either you start answering questions or you can hop out right now."

"Okay, fine!" he said.

I stared at him a few more seconds, then pulled into traffic again—not a popular decision with the other drivers. "Quit your honking!" I yelled out the window.

I turned to Michael. "Start talking."

"My stepfather called Jimmy," he said.

"Why?"

"They're . . ." he started, but his face drifted toward his window.

"Michael!"

"They're concerned about me," he managed, as if I'd asked him to finish an unpleasant green vegetable.

"The Wanda thing?"

"And Jimmy told them about the dreams."

"God, what an old woman!"

We drove in silence for a while.

"Well, I *suppose* I can haul you up to Baltimore," I said.

"Thank you."

"But I've got a couple of conditions."

"Okay," he said, hesitantly.

"One: I want to know what the hell happened to you and Wanda. Where did you go?"

"I'm sorry about that," he said, again.

"Never mind that. Where'd you go?"

"Tyler."

"Tyler Elementary?"

He nodded.

Tyler is about a mile from Alexander High School.

"What the hell were you doing there?"

"We sat in the parking lot and talked," he said.

"How long?"

"A while—an hour, I guess."

"Yeah, right." I laughed. Wanda didn't talk to *anybody* for an hour.

"We did," he insisted.

"About what?"

"A lot of things."

"Did you talk about why you decided to play the trashy couple, then leave me stranded?" I asked.

"Actually, Wanda has an interesting theory about our characters," he said, beginning to flush.

"Oh yeah?"

"She thinks it was the house."

"What?"

"She thinks the house influenced our characters—that the house reflected what it's seen in the past," Michael said.

Hearing this felt like finding a big piece of fat in the meat I was chewing.

"The house made you do it," I said.

"Right," he said, heating up. "See, Wanda doesn't pick out her characters ahead of time."

"I know," I said.

"She said she decided on one in the car, but then, right before we went in, something pushed that character out of the way. I felt it, too. Right when she was touching my hair."

"So, *the house* decided for you?"

"We think maybe it's seen the same old thing over and over again," he said. "Maybe it only knows one way."

"*We?*"

He nodded. "There's a behavioral theory about kids who've been abused—that even after they're out of the abusive situation, they're always trying to recreate it. Supposedly, their brains are unconsciously trying to work out what happened in the past and looking for a way to master the situation. They're trying to find a way to win."

"The house is trying to win?" I said sourly.

"Maybe it's trying to make sense of its memories," he said. "Would you want all that negative energy inside you?"

"Michael, houses are wood and glass and plaster someone nailed together! They aren't alive!"

"But don't you think it's possible that we give a house some kind of life by breathing and eating and dreaming inside it?"

"No!"

We were quiet for a moment.

"Why couldn't you just have fooled around like normal people?" I asked.

Michael didn't say anything, but I could tell he was staring at me. Since Michael never looked at anyone longer than absolutely necessary, I was a little surprised when I glanced over and he didn't look away. In fact, he stared so long, I finally gave in.

"What?"

"What do you believe in?" he asked.

"Santa."

"I'm serious. I want to know what you believe in."

I sighed.

"You make me answer all your questions," he said. "Now I want you to answer some of mine."

"What if I say no?"

"Then you can just drop me off here."

"On the side of the highway?"

"Yes. And don't—don't come around anymore."

I turned toward him, but his face looked like it usually did—an easy target for anything I wanted to throw at it.

I absolutely hated the idea of giving in to him, but Michael was the kind of person who *would* stroll down the side of a major highway at night. I imagined the headlights bouncing off his backpack as it bobbed up and down on the side of the road.

Then I thought of all the guys who'd be *real* interested in giving Michael a lift. I was going to have to break one of my rules and give him a look at the real me. I didn't think I could fake my way through.

"I don't know," I finally said. "Me, I guess."

"What?"

"Me. I believe in me."

"But what does that mean?"

"It means I know I'm smarter than most of the idiots out there," I said. "Maybe not smarter, but I know how to play them. I know how to work people. I know how to get what I want."

"And that's important to you?"

"Of course it is."

"So what are you going to do? What are you going to be?" he pressed.

"Happy and successful."

"And you're happy now? The way you are?"

"No, not perfectly happy," I said. "I'm still in high school . . . I don't have my own car yet."

"So there's still something missing," he said, like a detective catching the witness in a lie.

"Of course there is. I'm not eighteen yet. I don't have my own place."

"And once you—?"

"Yes, Michael, once I have those things, I'll be perfectly happy," I said. "And I know what you're going to say, so don't say it. You're going to tell me how shallow and materialistic I am. Well, you know what? You're right. But you know what else? I'm okay with that."

"What about people?"

"What about them? I have plenty of friends right now," I said. "Too many, actually. I probably need to get rid of a few."

It was supposed to be a joke, but it didn't sound even remotely funny.

"What about someone significant? Someone you're afraid to lose?" Michael said. "Are you going to be perfectly happy all by yourself?"

"I am now, so why shouldn't I be?"

He was staring again. I let him take a good long look. What did I care?

"You know what you are?" he finally said.

"What?"

"You're a grifter."

"A what?"

"A grifter. A con man."

"Bullshit."

"You're a grifter," he insisted. "You just said you know how to play people. It's a game to you. Everything's a scheme to get what you want."

"Whatever."

"Then maybe it's entertainment. Is that what you're looking for?"

"Shut up, Michael. I'm not looking for anything. I'm just trying to help you."

"But what are you getting out of it?" he asked.

"A massive pain in the ass."

I couldn't help remembering the imaginary interview on my first walk home from Michael's house—my conversation with the press about the good deed I was performing by helping this poor nerd.

"I'm just trying to help you, Michael, but if you don't want me around, I'll be more than happy to disappear."

No response. I smiled a little.

But just as I was beginning to calm down, he said, "Maybe it would be better."

"What was that?"

"Maybe it would be better if you . . . if we didn't hang out anymore."

We were closing in on Baltimore now.

"Fine with me. I guess that means I'm not your chauffeur anymore," I said. "Maybe I should just turn around and head back home."

"Can you still drop me off?"

"Why should I?"

"You owe me. You used me."

"Used you?!" I yelled. I was *really* mad now.

"Or am I some kind of charity project?" said Michael.

"You're some kind of idiot."

"Or maybe I'm just practice—maybe I'm some kind of grifting experiment for you."

"I'm trying to help you, dumb-ass!"

"You could have just been my friend. That would have helped."

"I am your friend," I said. Michael didn't say anything.

"Did you hear me?"

"Do you always call your friends 'dumb-ass' and 'idiot'?"

"When they're acting like it, yes."

We retreated to our corners.

I was done with Michael, I decided. Here I was, hauling him up to his father's crack house, and he had the nerve to tell me I was some kind of grifter? How much time had I spent with him? How many hours of social work had I performed on his behalf? I glared at Michael, ready to unload, but he was turned toward the window.

I clamped my jaw shut and stewed for the next twenty minutes. Although I'm sure it doesn't seem like it, twenty minutes feels like a lifetime if you're trapped in a car with someone you want to punch. At about the ten-minute mark, I almost started talking to him again, but then he coughed and the noise irritated me. I squeezed the hell out of the steering wheel until we found the right exit, turned off the highway, and headed into the city.

"You're going to have to help now," I said, tersely.

"Okay."

In an effort not to slap Michael every time he gave me a direction, I studied the city, looking for the line—the division—between urban and urban blight.

It was even harder to spot at night. You could find something sketchy anywhere you looked: the guy on the sidewalk talking to himself; two guys hustling down the front steps of a building and into the middle of the road; someone coming out after them.

I decided to look at buildings instead of people, hoping I'd see something familiar. The convenience stores we passed seemed to have more people hanging out in the parking lot than I remembered. Instead of one or two knots, there were several, and each knot seemed bigger and much more energetic than those of the day-shifters. The people looked looser, more comfortable, as if the sun was a bully who'd moved on to his next set of victims.

I tried to stop stewing about Michael's latest statements by deciding to give him a nice kick in the ass when we got out of the car.

I passed his father's place and kept going.

"I think you—"

"I know," I said. I hooked a U-turn in the middle of the street and headed back.

I took a right at the first cross street and found a good-sized gap between a couple of cars. Michael started to bail as I was trying to correct my pathetic attempt at parallel parking. "Well, thanks for the ride," he said.

"I'm not leaving you here."

"Why not?"

"What if your dad's not home?"

Michael stared.

"Did you call him?"

He nodded.

"And?" I demanded.

"No one picked up," he said. "But Chrissy's probably home."

"Yeah, but what if she isn't? What if nobody's home? You gonna hang out at the convenience store?"

He shrugged.

I closed my eyes and bounced my head against the steering wheel a few times. Michael saw his opportunity and slipped out the door.

"Oh no you don't, you little shit . . ." I muttered, scrambling out behind him.

I caught up with him at the second door—the one with the buttons.

"What are you doing?" he asked.

"Making sure you don't end up wandering the streets."

"Worried about losing your experiment?"

"Shut up."

He pushed the button for his father's apartment. Someone buzzed us in almost immediately. Michael barged through the second door and headed up the stairs, knocking into a big guy in a long, black coat.

"What the fuck?" the guy said, stopping.

"Sorry," I said. "My brother has trouble with doors. He's . . . special."

"Whatever," the guy huffed, shoving past me.

I hurried up the stairs after my special brother. The hallways weren't deserted like last time. People were coming and going, walking the corridors and hanging out by the stairs.

We passed one lovely couple on the second floor landing. The girl was in a corner, her boyfriend a few inches from her. He had her penned in, arms straight out and pressed against the wall. They looked as if they were either going to make out or start throwing punches. I guessed it was love. The guy glared at us as we passed. I nodded and kept moving.

The third floor was empty, but it felt like only like a lull in traffic.

Music still blared from every other door. Different genres competed for space in the cat-piss air. I followed Michael down the hall. He pushed through his father's unlocked apartment door. I stayed in the doorway.

The music was loud. His dad was just inside and to the left, sitting on the battered couch. He had an album cover on his lap and a beer in one hand.

"Hi," Michael said, nowhere near loud enough to get his father's attention.

His father didn't look up.

"Michael?" I said. Reaching for him, I tapped his shoulder.

He shrugged me off. I tried to grab his shirt, but he stepped out of reach and into the living room. He stopped a few feet from his father, staring down at him. His father looked up, squinted for a moment, then went back to his album cover.

Okay, that wasn't so bad. Maybe he's okay. Maybe he's just having a quick beer.

But in the pit of my stomach, I knew his father was well past number one. He should have been surprised to see Michael, but wasn't.

Michael's father looked up again and waved Michael closer.

As quietly as I could, I pulled the apartment door tight behind me. I couldn't tell if Michael's father had seen me yet and held on to the knob and the slim hope he hadn't.

I wondered where Chrissy was and felt a weird urge to make sure she was okay.

Michael stood over his father.

"Look at him," his father said, pointing to someone on the album cover. "How old do you think he is?"

Michael bent a little closer.

I was reluctant to leave the safety of the door but found myself sliding to my left to see if I could get a peek.

The album was old but not ancient. There were five or six guys lined up and leaning against what looked to be an old warehouse. Their clothes would pass as "retro" today. A young and energetic hipster would kill for a set or two.

The guys on the front didn't look old, but they didn't look that young, either—at least a few years older than Michael and I. Two had blond hair that was almost white, and they looked enough alike that I assumed they were brothers. The other guys had long hair and beards that hadn't seen a comb or cutting in a while.

"What do you think?" his father asked, looking up.

Michael shrugged, keeping his eyes away from his father's.

I took a few quiet side steps back toward the front door.

"He looks young, right? He looks like he's still in high school, doesn't he?"

"I guess so."

"But listen to that voice," his father said, getting excited. "Listen to it!"

I listened to the voice coming from the stereo. It didn't sound like a kid's. It sounded like some old man who'd smoked about a million packs of cigarettes.

"How does a kid sound like that?" his father demanded.

I could see only the side of his face, but his eyes were wide and looked full of something that wanted to leap out.

His father leaned forward and set the beer on the floor.

Michael flinched as his father jumped up from the couch, still holding the cover.

"I mean, look at 'em. They all look like kids! Probably were . . . back then."

Michael nodded, but he was looking at me, not at the album cover. I pointed to the beer on the floor.

"How does a kid have that much inside? He sings like he's a hundred. Wait! Listen to this part," his father said, putting a hand on Michael's shoulder, closing his eyes, and nodding to the beat. Suddenly, the singer broke in with a tremendous yell.

"That's what I'm talking about!" his father yelled back. "Now listen. You gotta hear the guitar coming up. It's unbelievable."

We waited for the guitar.

"There it is! Listen to how raw that is. It's like he's cutting his guts out!"

He closed his eyes again, contorting his face as if the sounds were painful. Michael looked to me for help. I pointed toward the back of the apartment. I wanted to check on Chrissy.

Michael didn't understand.

I pointed again, more emphatically this time, like he might suddenly understand if I used a little more force.

It didn't work.

"Check this out," his father said, suddenly coming out of his trance and pointing to a speaker. He listened to a few notes and closed his eyes again.

I darted for the hall.

There were two doors on the left and one on the right. Only one of them was closed, so I knocked.

"Go away, Daddy. You're not supposed to come in, remember?"

"It's Matthew . . ."

Five seconds.

"Who?"

"Michael's friend . . . Remember? Michael? Your . . . sort of brother?"

Seven seconds.

"I did a lot of laughing? Last time I was here?"

Four seconds, then a giggle.

"Can I come in?"

I pressed my ear to the door, hoping to hear something over the music, and wasn't ready when the door suddenly flew open. I stumbled forward, got tangled up in Chrissy, and took her down with me.

I got up as quickly as I could, imagining Michael's father in the doorway looking down at us. Chrissy just laughed.

"All right now, we can't start that again," I said, looking around. "Wow. Cool posters."

There were poster-sized comic book pages on her bedroom walls. It looked like I'd stumbled into the wing of a tiny art gallery. Each poster was framed, and each had a signature or a message in one corner or another.

"Daddy gets them at work. Mine's over there," she said, pointing.

"You drew one?"

She laughed. "No. *Mine's* over there."

I didn't get it, so I walked over for a closer look.

This one had more frames, and they were smaller—just enough room to tell a quick, easy story. I skimmed the panels. Chrissy and her father in some kind of studio or workroom. Chrissy sitting near a desk, playing with stuffed animals. Chrissy notices a fish tank by a window and moves in for a closer look. While she's admiring the sea horses, a monster (not too scary) kicks down the door to the studio and tries to abduct her father. Chrissy uses some kind of laser vision and turns the monster into an adorable stuffed animal.

"Cool," I said. "Who did it?"

"Byron."

I almost asked who Byron was, but didn't see the point. Instead, I took a quick look around.

Chrissy had a big bed. The comforter was super-girly: whites and pinks and tons of frilly crap along every available edge. Her bed looked like a giant birthday cake. There were stuffed animals neatly arranged across the pillows and a matching bureau and table pushed against a wall.

The table had a big oval mirror attached to the top. Like the bed-spread, the furniture was girly, and like the bedspread, it seemed a little out of place in a teenager's room.

"Why are you hanging out in here?" I asked.

She sat on the edge of her bed, not looking at me.

"Daddy's drinking," she said.

"Why?"

"He's sad."

"He is?"

"About Michael."

"Why's he sad about Michael?" I asked.

She shrugged. Something occurred to me.

"When did he start drinking again?"

"Right after you two idiots showed up," her father said. He was in the doorway now, beer in hand.

I could see Michael just behind him, his pale, worried face trying to peer around his father's large frame. I had a little trouble finding the right words. After all, Michael's father had just called me an idiot.

"Sorry," was all I could come up with.

Helpful Hint When Dealing with the Drunk: I've dealt with intoxicated friends on a number of occasions. When it comes to drunks, the best thing you can do is say as little as possible and keep things neutral. You never know what's going to set them off.

"Yeah, you should be," he said, taking a swig. "Whose fucking idea was it to come find Dad anyway?"

"Mine," I said.

He sipped his beer and looked around the room.

"Did you do all these comics?" I asked. Though quick to anger, drunks can usually be re-directed fairly easily.

"I worked on most of 'em."

"Did you do the one about Chrissy?"

He smiled. "Nah, that was Byron Thomas. You heard of Byron Thomas?"

I shook my head.

"One of the best artists in the business right now. One of the best *ever*, actually. Nicest guy you'll ever meet, too. Chrissy loved to hang around his desk."

He walked into the room. Michael stayed in the doorway. I sidled over to Michael while his father studied the poster.

"I should have colored these a little differently," he said, pointing.

"Oh yeah?" I said. Then, under my breath to Michael: "Michael, you're not staying here tonight."

"Okay," he said.

I hadn't expected him to give in so easily.

"See this? This here?" his father was saying. "Brilliant. No one else would have done it that way."

"We need to leave soon," I whispered.

"I know," Michael said.

"That's what he's known for," his father continued, "but it's not a gimmick. He's always got a good reason for drawing a scene a certain way. Get over here, you two," he said, motioning with his beer.

We squeezed in beside him. Chrissy stood on her bed, looking over his shoulder. She seemed confused. I assumed she wasn't used to having her father in her room when he was drinking.

Michael's father pointed to an early frame, one of Chrissy playing by a desk.

"Chrissy always sat near Byron's desk when I took her to work with me. Used to take her toys over there and play. You remember that, hon?"

She nodded carefully.

"She'd prop her stuffed animals up against Byron's desk and lay a big piece of paper on the floor in front of her. She used to pretend she was working."

He stared at the poster.

Okay, that was a lovely little story. Very heartwarming. Maybe he's in a better mood now. Maybe it's time to yawn and stretch and look at our watches.

"Then he screwed us and went to Marvel," said Michael's father. "I should throw it out the fucking window."

"No, Daddy!" Chrissy yelled.

"I didn't say I was going to. Smarten up, will you?"

Chrissy sat down on the bed, scowling.

"I am smart," she said.

Her father sighed and closed his eyes. Then he put a hand on her shoulder. She tried to shake it off.

"I know you're smart, honey," he said. "I'm sorry. I wasn't mad at you. You know that."

"You shouldn't be in here," she said. "You're not allowed in here when you're drinking."

"I know, honey. What if I leave right now? Will you still be mad?"

Reluctantly, she shook her head.

"Thank you, Beautiful," he said, then kissed the top of her head. He moved toward us and pointed toward the front of the apartment.

We ended up in the living room. The record had ended, and Michael's father hovered over the stacks, looking for another. I nudged Michael.

"What?"

I nodded toward his father and opened my eyes as far as they would go.

"Oh."

"There it is," his father said, grinning. "That's the one." He brought another album up to the turntable.

"Ah . . . Dad?" Michael tried.

"You guys ever hear of John Paul Clue-So?" his father asked.

Or at least that's what it sounded like to me. It was some French-sounding name, so if anybody knows who he was talking about, feel free to let me know. Actually, don't. I don't really care.

"No," we said.

"Jazz violinist?" he tried.

We shook our heads.

"Damn," he said happily, shaking his head. "I can't believe you've never heard of him."

He handed the album cover to Michael, changed records, and dropped the needle. Michael pretended to study the cover. The music wasn't bad, but I had my mind on other things.

"So in the early '70s, there was this movement in jazz toward—"

"Dad, we have to go," Michael said.

I closed my eyes. *Why is there never any tact?*

His father didn't seem too happy about the interruption. "What do you mean?" he said. "It's not even nine yet."

"I've got school tomorrow," Michael said.

"Yeah, me too," I agreed, hoping his father didn't suddenly remember it was Friday.

"So?"

"It's kind of a long trip back," I said.

"It's like forty minutes," his father said.

"I've still got some homework to finish," I said.

"So? Skip it."

I was temporarily out of excuses.

"Come on," his father said. "Just stay another hour. We'll listen to a few tunes, then you can go."

"Michael's got to meet someone," I said, recovering.

"Do you now?" his father said, raising his eyebrows.

"Yeah, Michael doesn't like to piss her off, do you Michael?"

Michael shook his head emphatically.

His father rolled his eyes. "Michael, let me give you a little advice about women," he said.

We pretended to listen to a five-minute lecture on the way a "man" is expected to act in a relationship. It isn't worth repeating.

"Yeah, well, anyway, Michael likes her, so we have to get going," I said. "I guess she lets him touch her or something."

His father laughed. Michael frowned.

"All right, then. I guess I understand," his father said.

He grabbed my hand and shook it. He turned to Michael, hand outstretched, but suddenly had an idea. "Hey, wait a minute. I've got something for you," he said. He set his beer by the couch and hurried back to the records. Michael glared at me.

"Well, it's getting us out of here, isn't it?" I said.

We spent an uncomfortable minute watching his father flip through albums, talking to himself the whole time. Things like: "Oh, yeah, got to have that one. That one's a classic." Finally, he hurried over with an armload of records. "For you," he said, shoving them into Michael's arms.

"I don't have a record player."

"Get one from a yard sale or something. Actually, they're starting to make 'em again. People are coming back to analog. It's much warmer than digital and—"

"I've got one you can have," I offered, hoping to head off another lecture.

"See? There you go," his father said, satisfied.

"Why are you giving them to me?" Michael asked.

"And say hi to your girlfriend for me," his father said with a smirk. "Man, I'm glad Chrissy won't have a boyfriend. Couldn't deal with that."

Somewhere in the apartment, a door slammed.

"Ah, shit!" his father said, covering his eyes with a hand. "Thank God I've only got one kid," he said, heading down the hall. "Two would've killed me."

I stood in the middle of the mess Michael's father had made, too stunned to say anything right away. "Well, I guess we should go," I said, listening to his father rap on Chrissy's door.

"Come on, Chrissy, open up. I didn't say that right. Let me explain."

"Yeah, I guess we should probably get going," I mumbled, looking at Michael's feet. I tried to glance at his face but couldn't deal with what I saw. I ended up back at his feet. I'm still not sure whether he dropped them intentionally or they just slipped, but I figured our time was up when the records hit the floor.

I led the way out the door and down the hall to the stairs. I suddenly remembered the lovely couple from earlier and wondered if they were still on the landing.

Thankfully, they'd moved on. Maybe they'd found a nicer floor. Or a roomier stairwell. I didn't care. I just wanted to get outside. I tried to worry about the car but couldn't work up the energy. My brain felt like a bridge well past its weight limit.

I wove my way through some people near the front door, ignored a few comments, and found myself outside on the sidewalk. I turned to wait for Michael, but he was right on my heels. He brushed past me without a word. His cheeks were flushed and his eyes . . . well, I don't really have the words to describe them.

The car looked okay, but even if we'd found it with one tire, no doors, and a fire in the backseat, I still would have tried to drive home.

Michael's father and this city could go to hell.

I pulled away from the curb and headed out.

Driving away from that apartment building felt like finding the surface after a long, frightening swim under the ice.

* * *

We didn't speak on the ride home. Michael finally broke the silence when I dropped him off in front of his house.

"Thanks," he said.

"No problem," I said. "I figure I'll have my chauffeur's license pretty soon and I can start charging."

"Not for the ride," he said.

I waited.

"Thanks for showing me my mom's not a liar."

"What?"

"Thanks for showing me my father the drunk."

"Michael . . ."

He slammed the door. I watched him work his way around the junkyard in the driveway and through the side door. The lights were on inside. I wondered if Flap was still there. I wondered if they were up, waiting for him.

For their sake, I hoped not.

CHAPTER 14

After pulling into the garage, I killed the engine, and sat for a minute, thinking.

Thinking about the night and how every part of it had been a piece of crap. Wishing I had turned off the phone and crawled into bed at 7:00.

Unlocking the door to the house, the last thing I needed was a chatty parent.

I opened it as quietly as possible. There was a light on in the kitchen. *Damn it.*

A crappy end to a shitty evening.

"So, where'd you go?"

"I took my new friend Michael up to Baltimore to see his biological father."

"Sounds like fun! Did you guys have a good time?"

"His dad was drunk and acted like a tool."

"Oh, that's great! Good for you."

I slipped out of my shoes and resigned myself to the brief walk to the kitchen. Maybe I'd just wave and swing upstairs. I stopped a few yards shy and listened.

No sounds, no voice requesting my presence for a debriefing. I took the last few steps.

No Mom.

"Thank *God*," I muttered.

I couldn't tell if she'd simply stepped out of the room or hadn't been in it for a while. I wanted something to drink, but had to weigh the desire against an unexpected opportunity to make it to my room unmolested.

Hanging around for even a minute seemed like pushing my luck, and tonight felt like a bad night for that. I looked for any signs of recent activity.

In a little clearing between two piles, I noticed a mug and a plate. The plate held the tattered remains of some bread or pastry. There was only an inch or so of liquid in the mug. No steam.

Could she actually be in bed?

I decided to risk it.

Bathroom, I decided, getting myself a glass of juice. *She's probably in the bathroom.*

I took a sip, listening, but downstairs really did feel empty.

At least I've managed to catch one break tonight.

I left the empty glass on the counter and, starting for the stairs, felt the need to stop as I passed the table.

Toast, I decided, looking down at the plate. *Coffee*, I decided, peering at the mug. *Possibly chai?*

Who the hell cares? Let's go!

But I didn't. Instead, I found myself lingering at the edge of the table, on the cusp of remembering something.

The papers.

I smiled. Mom's secret papers—the ones she'd shoved under a pile before I could get a look at them.

I reached for the pile and lifted the corner, pulling the bottom third closer.

Disappointing. The top few pages were nothing but columns of numbers below headings that made no sense. I toyed with the idea of "accidentally" spilling the rest of Mom's coffee over a pile or two.

Looking through the rest of the pile, I found a stapled set at the very bottom. These were different. The paper was longer and there was a seal near the bottom of the first page. I became a bit more interested when I saw my last name scattered here and there across the length of the document.

I began to read. About halfway through, I sat down.

I shoved the plate and mug to one side. The toast ended up on the table. I left it.

I skimmed the document once, stopping to read here and there. Then

I read it again, slowly.

It was pretty self-explanatory. Mom wanted to separate from Dad.

I sat for a minute, thinking, then slipped the papers back into place. I straightened the stack, then gently pulled the mug and plate back to their former positions. I replaced the toast and carefully swept the crumbs into the palm of my hand.

I stood by the trash a while, brushing the crumbs from my hands. Thinking.

I crossed the room, hooking the keys over their ring. I started up the first few stairs and stopped. I stood for a moment, then came back down and into the kitchen.

At the edge of the table, I found the right pile and pulled out the set of papers again.

I walked over to the trash can.

I stood over the papers, considering, then pushed them down, hard. I pulled some soggy plastic and used napkins over the top for good measure.

Rinsing my hands, killing the lights, and climbing the stairs.

Getting undressed and slipping into bed.

Feeling . . . grateful—grateful that I didn't feel a damn thing.

In fact, I started to fall away the minute my head hit the pillow.

After a time, I heard someone walking downstairs and didn't think twice about it.

Falling asleep and refusing to wonder whose footsteps. Because it didn't matter. It didn't matter if they went from the living room to the kitchen.

Why should it?

Michael and his father tried to bother me for a while, but I wasn't about to let them. There was nothing to keep me from falling asleep, just like I always did.

One last attempt: Michael's voice, just before I fell.

Saying just one word: "grifter."

His voice came and went, leaving me completely alone.

CHAPTER 15

Saturday morning came. I slept in.

And when I finally admitted to myself that trying to doze off one more time was a lost cause, guess what?

I was *still* finished with Michael.

I stretched but didn't get up.

I'd poured a ridiculous amount of time, energy, and expertise into him . . . and what had he given me in return?

Nothing. Not even a few bucks for gas money.

Just a lot of trouble topped with attitude.

I will admit it: I was reluctant to close the book on him completely. There was one last piece of information I wanted. I wanted to know what happened after I dropped him at his house Saturday night, but I wasn't about to ask. I knew Michael would try to apologize to me at some point, and when he did, I'd extract the information and dismiss him for good.

I'd keep an eye open for him at school on Monday, but I wouldn't go out of my way to find him.

Why should I?

I'd tried to help Michael and he screwed it all up.

Actually, considering the size of the battle and the stupidity of my subject, I felt like I'd done an admirable job.

And when you think about it, I *was* fairly successful. Because of *me*, Michael's life was far better than it had been, both at school and probably at home.

Michael was no longer at the bottom of the food chain. He wasn't anywhere near the top (like me), but he'd definitely come up from the bottom of the ocean. Michael got considerably less shit from the general public than he ever had. In fact, more than a few people thought he was a badass.

And he'd finally seen his father again. Granted, it hadn't gone as well as I'd anticipated, but still, at least he'd been up to see him.

And Wanda! If you could believe Michael's version of "The Parking Lot," Wanda might actually want to see him again.

(Which reminded me, I still needed to have a talk with her about ditching me.)

And that whole "grifter" thing? I think Michael's full of shit. If I'm such a con artist, then what the hell did I get out of our "friendship"?

So it was settled: With the exception of a few minutes to hear his apology, no more Michael. He was officially dismissed, and the dismissal felt good.

But even I had to admit, while he was a massive pain in the ass, he'd temporarily helped to alleviate some of the monotony of school. Now that he was gone, I would need another distraction.

I suppose that's why I started thinking about Chrissy.

Or maybe I wanted to prove Michael wrong and show everyone (once again) what a helpful young man I am.

I don't really know, but whatever the reason, she kept coming up that morning as I started thinking about a new distraction. And when she did, it was almost always the comment her father had dropped—the one about her not having a date or a boyfriend or whatever he'd said. Don't ask me why. After all, I'm sure she'd heard far worse when he was hammered.

Even though Michael had been a huge expenditure of time and effort, I was now rolling out of bed and into the shower, on the verge of making my second trip to Baltimore in less than twenty-four hours.

Getting the car again wasn't a problem. When I came downstairs, Mom's car was in the garage, although she was nowhere to be found (not that I made much of an effort to find her).

Who knew where Dad was.

Driving up to Baltimore, I hoped that Michael's father was working on a nice hangover. I figured persuading him to let Chrissy out of his sight for two minutes would be much easier if his brain wasn't firing on all cylinders.

It was kind of nice going up in the middle of the day: sunny, and not much traffic. And even if they were out, or he wouldn't let me see her, at least it felt like I was doing *something* to counter the unpleasant aftertaste of "The Michael Affair."

I hadn't bothered to pull up the directions. I was in a hurry and figured I could probably remember them—the last visit was still pretty fresh. Coasting down their street, I looked hard for the line. Once again, however, I missed it. I got distracted by a weird-looking bug on the dashboard, and when I was finally able to shoo it out the passenger-side window, I had already crossed.

My memory is always pretty reliable, and in no time I was pulling up in front of their apartment. I was halfway to the door when I remembered I should be parking on a side street. It took some of the spring out of my step, but it didn't take long to find a better spot and resume my approach. I was almost to the building when another bothersome thought cropped up. The security door.

Although it hadn't been a problem on our last two visits, I wondered if Dad would be a little less inclined to let people in this morning. *Oh well. I'm here. Might as well try.*

I pushed the button.

Nothing.

Great.

I tried the door, then leaned in closer, wondering if anyone was on the other side. I couldn't see much. The hallway was dark and the glass was filthy. I almost had a heart attack when the door suddenly flew open.

A skinny little guy stopped, gave me a quick look up and down, and held the door open for me.

"Forget your key?" he said.

"Yeah. Thanks."

"I hate this fucking door," he said.

"You're not the only one," I said, disappearing inside.

So much for security.

They might not be home, but at least I'd know for sure. But just as I rounded the first landing, I stopped in my tracks.

Something occurred to me.

What if they *were* home but couldn't hear the buzzer? What if Dad was having a few beverages and listening to some tunes?

I closed my eyes, groaned, and dragged my legs up the rest of the steps. No time for self-pity. I needed to plan. What would I do if Dad was drunk? Listen to the beginning of the music lecture, then bolt for the door? And what about Chrissy? Would she know I tried to see her, or would she have locked herself in the bedroom?

I made it to the third floor and headed down the hall with my head cocked to one side. Music came through some of the doors, but it was low and cautious, as if it knew someone had a hangover. I heard some TVs and a few voices, but a lot of the apartments felt empty.

I stopped in front of Michael's father's door and put an ear to the wood.

No music, but that didn't mean I was in the clear. A picture came to me, of Michael's father standing eagerly on the other side of the door, records in hand, just waiting for me to knock.

I chased the image away and tapped on the wood.

No one answered, but I knew I needed to give it a real try. I stepped forward with my arm in the air, but before I could knock, the door swung in. I let Michael's father stare at my arm for a few seconds before I realized I wouldn't need its services.

"How'd you get in?" he asked.

"They know me here."

His eyebrows bunched up, but he didn't say anything.

"So, how's it going?" I asked casually.

He was in a dirty white robe and hadn't brushed his hair. He looked like he'd seen better days.

"Is Michael with you?" he asked, out into the hall.

"Nope."

His father nodded but kept his eyes away from mine.

"Kind of quiet in there," I said. "No music today?"

Definitely the wrong thing to say, but I hadn't given myself enough prep time.

"Yeah, Chrissy told me you guys were here," he said tightly.

"She told you?" I said.

"Memory problems," he said, tapping his temple and giving me a grimace.

I nodded.

"Did I . . .?" he started, but couldn't finish.

"You mean last night?"

He nodded.

"You were all right," I said. "You just talked a lot about music."

He shook his head from side to side.

"You tried to give us some of your albums."

"I did?"

It was like talking to one of my friends: *"Dude, I was completely wasted last night. Did I do anything stupid?"*

"No, you were all right. Don't worry, everyone throws up in their drive-way, then somersaults through it."

"Did Michael . . . I mean, was Michael upset?"

"A little. But he'll get over it."

Michael's father closed his eyes and sighed. "You don't know what it feels like—what it did to me to see him again," he said.

"I wouldn't worry about it," I said, but only because I wanted him to stop. Then I saw my chance. "I'm pretty sure he'll be back," I said. "But you *were* kind of mean to Chrissy."

"How?" he demanded.

"You said something about how you were glad she wouldn't ever have a date. You didn't say it to her face, but she was listening."

"So that's why she's so mad," he said, as if I'd solved a gigantic mystery for him.

"That's why I'm here," I announced. "I'm going to take her out."

He took his time digesting the words.

"What do you mean?"

I tried to look behind him. No Chrissy, but that didn't mean she wasn't around.

"Not a real date," I said, quietly. "Just out for a while."

"I don't think so."

"Why not?"

"Because I don't even know you," he said. "I'm not going to let my daughter go out with some kid I don't even know."

"How is that different than some guy from her school taking her out?"

"For one thing, you're older than she is," he said. "And why the hell are you doing this anyway?"

"I'm not that much older," I said.

It was pretty lame, I realize, but what do you want? I was improvising.

"No," he said, shaking his head. "No way."

"Why not?"

"I just told you."

"So you're just going to keep her locked up forever?"

"Maybe. It's none of your business what I do," he said, getting pissy.

I had to tone it down or he'd shut that door for good.

"Sorry," I said. "Look, I know it's not my business, but what are you worried about? You don't think I'm going to try something, do you?"

He kind of snorted and grimaced at the same time.

"We'll just go to the aquarium for a while—she likes sea horses, right?" I said, remembering the poster. "And people are always getting hysterical about how great the aquarium is here."

"So I'm just supposed to give you a few bucks and tell you kids to have a good time?"

"I've got money," I said, even though I knew that wasn't the point.

"Look, I already said no, so I don't know why we're still talking about this."

The door was about to close.

That's when I suddenly imagined Michael standing beside me. He put a hand on my shoulder and nodded encouragingly. The image was going to make me either laugh or vomit all over Dad.

"Something funny?" his father asked.

"Sorry. Just thinking about something Michael said."

"About me?"

"No, no . . . something we were talking about the other day."

He stared at me and said, "Well, anyway, I'm sorry you drove all the way up here."

It only took a second to decide. I knew what would get me in, and although it wasn't something I intended to submit for end-of-day announcements at school, if there was ever a time to play the card, this was it. Besides, who cared if Michael's drunk father knew? After all, he'd probably flush the new information out during the next good bender.

"Look, you don't need to worry about me . . . about me trying anything. I think I might be gay."

I watched his father's face. He definitely wasn't expecting the information he'd just received.

"What do you mean?" he finally asked.

"I think I prefer boys instead of girls."

"I know what it means," he said, uncomfortably.

I didn't point out that he was the one who'd asked.

"You don't . . . have anything, do you?" his father asked.

"What?" *Have anything? What's he asking for? Beer? Meth?*

"Nothing. Never mind," he said.

He looked me over again. There was something about the way he did it that reminded me of Michael—the way he'd looked into me just before he let go and told me about his dreams.

So I let him. I figured I had nothing to lose. I didn't have much left to try anyway—just a push-him-down-and-run-into-Chrissy's-room plan, and I wasn't big on that one.

"So where did you say you wanted to go?" he asked.

And that was that.

As soon as I stepped into the apartment, Chrissy's door suddenly closed.

"Must be windy in here," I said, hustling down the hall before he could change his mind.

"Yeah," he said, watching me go.

I knocked on her door.

"What?"

"Hi, Chrissy. It's Matthew."

Three seconds.

"Who?"

"Matthew. Michael's friend?"

Two seconds.

"Hi."

"Hi," I said. "Can I come in?"

"I guess so."

She was sitting on the bed, trying to look as if she hadn't been listening.

"What's up?" I said, sitting down next to her.

"Nothing."

She was a little red and wouldn't look at me.

"You look guilty," I said. "You hiding some guy in here?"

"No," she almost shouted. She was smiling now.

"You probably have plans today, huh?"

Five seconds. "What?"

"You're probably busy today, huh? Probably doing something with one of your boyfriends?"

"I don't have *boyfriends,*" she said. It was the loud denial of an elementary school girl, secretly pleased that someone thought she was grown-up enough to have a boyfriend.

"Yeah, right. You might be able to fool your dad, but I know better."

She gave me a look. "Well, I don't," she said.

I studied the walls for a minute.

"Well, anyway, I was going to the aquarium today," I said. "I thought maybe you might want to come with me. If you're not doing anything."

She smiled down at her hands.

"Is my dad going?"

"I think he has a few things he wants to do. Is it okay if it's just you and me?"

Five seconds.

"How are we going to get there?"

"I brought my car," I said.

"You can drive?"

"Sort of."

She was quiet.

"Have you ever been there?" I asked.

She nodded.

"What do you like best?"

"The seahorses."

"They have seahorses there?" I pretended.

She stood up and launched into a dissertation on the seahorse: the different types, their preferred environment, their dietary needs, and a measured opinion of the cutest. I did my best to say, "Really?" and "Wow!" and "No way!"

(Did you know that the male seahorse carries the eggs in his pouch? I didn't.)

She sat down in front of her girly mirror to brush her hair, still talking. I looked over and saw her father in the doorway.

"She really likes seahorses," I said.

"Who knew?" he said, heading back to the living room.

The only break in her monologue occurred while she was putting on make-up—I watched her apply lipstick and use a little brush on her cheeks. I wondered where in the world she'd learned those tricks—probably not from Dad. I felt a little uncomfortable sitting and gawking at her, so I stood up and wandered toward the living room.

She was out before her father and I needed to make awkward conversation. I found myself caught up in her face for a moment and began to understand why he was all cramped-up about her going out with strange guys.

"So, what time would you like us back, sir?" I said, trying to sound like a nice young man.

Chrissy was standing a few feet away staring at the closed front door.

"How about three?"

"Four?"

His face got all frowny.

"Okay, three it is," I said. "You ready, Chrissy?"

Her face got red and she dropped her eyes, staring down at the floor. Not only did she look angry, she looked like Michael.

I tried to figure out if I'd said anything to upset her, but then her father saw his opportunity and ran with it.

"You don't have to go if you don't want to, honey," he said, quickly.

"We could probably go another time, maybe," I added, making sure the possibility seemed remote at best.

Chrissy was silent.

"It's a little too much for her right now," her father said to me, reaching for his daughter's hand. "Come on, hon, you can stay here with me."

She let him take her hand, but when he tried to lead her from the door, she shook herself loose.

"I'm going," she said, looking up at him.

"Are you sure, hon? Because you don't need to feel like—"

"Dad!"

"Okay, okay," he said, raising his hands in defeat.

Her face was flushed like Michael's, and her eyes had the same look he got when I pushed him too hard.

"Come on," she said, tugging me out the door.

"Back at three!" her father called after us.

"Four?" I tried, again.

"Three!"

Chrissy marched down the hallway without looking back. I followed her down the stairs and around the landings. She pushed her way through the doors and finally came to a stop when she realized her feet were on the sidewalk.

She was breathing hard. I hung back for a minute. If someone had come along at that moment, I'm sure they would have thought we'd had a fight and I was trying to get my girlfriend to come back inside.

I pulled up next to her.

"We don't have to go," I said. "I just thought you might like to get out for a while . . . you know, without your dad."

"I'm not scared," she said.

"I know you're not."

"And I'm not stupid," she said, turning on me. "You think I'm stupid."

"No I don't."

She turned away.

"I don't hang out with stupid people," I said. "Well, except for Michael."

I was hoping for a smile but didn't get one. I got this instead: "I'm not going to have sex with you."

"I don't . . . Why do you—? . . . I'm not . . ."

"I know a lot more than you think," she said.

"I'm sure you do."

She folded her arms and looked down at the sidewalk.

"Why did you come up here?" she asked.

"I just thought you might want to hang out. With someone your own age, I mean."

Why do I sound like a parent?

"You're older than me," she said.

"Not as old as your dad, though."

She nodded at the sidewalk.

"I have friends," she said. "At school."

"I'll bet you do."

"I'm not some retard just because I go to a different school."

"I know that."

"And I don't want to go if it's just one time."

"What do you mean?"

"I don't want to go if you're not coming back."

I felt a little stab in my chest and quickly shoved it into the smelly little bathroom in my head.

"I'll come back if you want me to," I said, weakly.

She studied my face, just like her father had, just like Michael had. I guess she was okay with what she found, because she suddenly turned back into a shy little girl.

"Where's your car?" she asked.

"It's right over there," I said, pointing to a parked police car across the street.

"You're not a cop," she said.

"Don't make me arrest you," I said, leading her around the corner and down the side street.

"Why aren't we going in your police car?" she said, smiling.

"I'm undercover," I said, unlocking the doors. "They need my help at the aquarium. Some kind of mystery."

"No they don't."

"I have a talking dog and a van," I said.

"No you don't."

She told me she knew the way.

"Sounds good," I said, wishing my phone wasn't in the glove compartment.

Looking at the clock, I realized it was lunchtime and I was starting to get hungry. Not a good thing. I get kind of pissy when I get hungry, so I was going to have to watch myself.

"They have a dolphin," she said, opening her window just a bit, then closing it again.

"Oh yeah?" I said, the same way I'd answer a little kid who told me she lived on an anthill.

"They do," she said, glaring.

Oops . . . I'm going to have to be careful.

"You mean like a stuffed dolphin or something?" I said.

"No. A real dolphin, in a swimming pool."

"Oh . . . Can you ride it?"

It took her a few seconds to process.

"What?"

"Why is it in a pool?" I said. "So people can ride it?"

Five seconds.

"You don't ride dolphins," she said.

"Do you eat them?"

"No!"

"I like swordfish," I said. "Is there a restaurant in the aquarium?"

She crossed her arms and glared out the window.

"Sorry," I said. "Just a little hungry. How many seahorses do they have?" I asked.

No response.

"I remember seeing something on the news about their seahorse collection," I said.

Five seconds.

"It's the biggest in the world," she said, still looking out the window.

"Not in the world," I said.

"Yes," she said, a little louder.

"So how many?"

"A hundred and eighty."

"No way!"

"Well, they're not all seahorses," she said, warming up a little. "They have sea dragons, too."

She was fine after that. I'd explain to you the difference between a seahorse and a sea dragon, but I stopped listening once I realized a sea dragon is about the same size as a seahorse. Anyway, I just wanted her in a good mood. Who wants to drag a pouty girl around all afternoon?

Eventually, we saw a few signs for the aquarium and followed them. I didn't want to pay a hundred dollars to park in the aquarium lot, so I was pretty happy when I found a spot nearby. Ten minutes after that and we were closing in on the harbor, on our way to the aquarium just like any other couple. I kind of liked the cover. I felt like shaking someone's hand.

Hello there, I'm Matthew, heterosexual male. This is my girlfriend, Chrissy.

She chattered about seahorses while I played tourist.

I perked up a little when I noticed the guys with silver food carts.

"Want a hot dog?" I said.

"No thanks," she said, slipping right back into her lecture.

I don't know what I was thinking. I really should have gotten some food, either at my house or on the way up. Even the gasoline/dead fish smell coming from the water was somewhat appetizing. But all too soon, we were taking a little footbridge over a slice of water that dropped us about fifty yards from the aquarium.

The building itself, unlike the others scattered nearby, was certainly . . . unique. At first glance, it looked as if the builders had accidentally collapsed the whole thing just as they were finishing up, then shoved the whole mess together before the boss could see. As we got closer, I decided the contractors involved in the waterfront renovation had used the site of the future aquarium as a junkyard. Then, once they were wrapping things up, someone realized they'd probably need to do *something* with all the extras—either slap them together or haul them out.

The solution: Bring in a giant crane, hire someone with very little time or patience, then slide, stack, and shove everything closer together and call it a building.

Standing in line for tickets, I stared up at a couple of glass triangles, several slabs of cement about the size and shape of a submarine, and a deflated trapezoid glued to the front for good measure.

Unique.

The line to buy tickets wasn't long, and we were inside before I had time to make a side trip to the nearest food cart. We talked a little, mostly about fish, but occasionally I was able to steer her toward something else. Like school.

"Do you like school?" I asked.

It was such a dumb question I almost punched myself in the face.

Was I some random adult trying to have an uncomfortable conversation with a teenager?

"Yeah," she said, "it's okay."

"What do you like about it?" I asked, again immediately disgusted with myself.

"I don't know."

"Are the kids nice?"

"Some."

"Are the teachers nice?"

"Yeah."

Okay, I was done, and I sure as hell wasn't going to throw out, "What's your favorite subject?"

"I haven't been held in over a year," she said.

"Oh yeah?"

What does that mean?

"Some kids get held every day," she added.

I guessed that being "held" wasn't like getting a hug.

"I don't get like that anymore," she said.

I wanted to pursue the holding thing, though it was a little unsettling, but I could tell she was done.

We spent some time outside, looking at the water. I liked it outside, near the open water, but Chrissy was anxious to get to the seahorse exhibit and we were back inside after ten minutes.

Considering her obsession with seahorses, I figured we'd be staring at them for the next three hours, but I was wrong. We started at a pretty good pace, and didn't stay long near any of the tanks.

Chrissy talked as she moved down the row of tanks, eyes pressed close. She talked, but she wasn't talking to me anymore. She was like an employee making her rounds. Actually, she was pretty good company. Sometimes she directed a comment to me, but most of the time, she seemed to be lecturing an imaginary group of tourists. And even when she was talking to me, it didn't seem to matter much if I responded or not.

After a while, my thoughts started to wander.

Chrissy had agreed to come on the condition that I'd make at least one follow-up visit. I started to plan. Should I take her to the aquarium again, or someplace different? Like Gut, Dad needed a little work, but I'd have to be careful; Dad would probably be a bit more challenging. He was definitely touchy, and touchy people are like an unfamiliar dog: ears cocked, blocking your way, just looking for a good reason to latch onto your forearm.

Lost in thought, and only half-listening, I trailed behind her.

"Why do they have you two together?" she said, leaning forward to examine a tank.

I glanced over but wasn't sure what she meant. A big chunk of reddish-pink coral accounted for almost every inch of space. I leaned forward but couldn't see anything.

"You don't like it in there."

Something in her voice tugged at my sleeve. It wasn't the words—it was the tone. There was something dangerous there, like a sliver of flame jumping to life near a baby's crib.

Chrissy was close to a tank, her index finger pressed against the glass, staring intently at something. I stepped up beside her.

"You don't like it in there," she repeated.

A very small seahorse clung to a thin branch of coral. Since the occupant didn't seem terribly upset, I searched the tank, looking for an explanation. Coral, gravel, seahorse—just like all the other tanks. What was the problem? Was the tank too small?

"Why doesn't he like it in there?" I asked.

"*She.*"

I sighed. "Okay, why doesn't *she* like it?"

Five seconds. No answer.

"Lonely?" I guessed.

Nothing.

"Hungry?"

I was thinking about hot dogs again when Chrissy stabbed the glass with a finger, hard, like she meant to break through it if she could.

"That one! That's why!"

I scanned the room. A few faces turned toward us. A guard at one end was suddenly interested. I looked at Chrissy, then back at the tank. Her finger was still jammed up against the side, the tip white from the pressure.

"What are you . . . What's wrong?" I asked.

"She *shouldn't* be *in* there with *that* one!" She punctuated the words *shouldn't, in,* and *that* with additional stabs at the glass.

More faces now, and a guard headed our way. I scanned the tank again, desperate for something, anything.

"I don't understand," I said. "What . . . ?"

And then I saw it: another, bigger seahorse just above the little one. Exactly the same color as the coral. Turned sideways, tail around a branch, and one chameleon eye pointed down at the little one. Sizing up its room-mate.

"Everything okay over here?" the guard asked.

I began to answer, but Chrissy broke in: "That little one shouldn't be in there with him."

The guard looked at Chrissy, paused, and bent forward, staring into the tank. "Hmm . . . I think you might be right," he said. "I'll let someone know, okay?"

"Thank you," I said, as if he and I both understood how difficult children could be.

The guard frowned at me, then turned back to Chrissy. "One of the biologists should be in soon. I'll make sure she takes a look as soon as she gets in, okay?"

Chrissy nodded, but her eyes never left the tank.

"Okay, well, thanks for your help," I said. "We'll try to keep our fingers off the glass. Right, Chrissy?"

No response. I smiled ruefully at the guard. He frowned.

"So. . ." I tried. "Maybe we should go see the . . . other stuff?"

I reached over, thinking I might take her elbow.

Didn't work.

She twisted away and continued her inspection, picking up right where she had left off. I followed at a safe distance, watching for any sudden movements. I'm not sure what I would have done if she had suddenly decided to sprint back to the other tank and free the threatened seahorse herself, but I sure as hell wasn't thinking about food anymore.

It seemed to take forever, but eventually, we found ourselves at the end of the exhibit.

"So," I said, "any more seahorses we need to . . . check on?"

She shook her head.

I looked at my watch, but I don't actually wear one, so I ended up looking at my wrist. "Your father wanted us back at two, right?" I said.

"Three."

Well, at least she's talking now.

"Anything else we have to . . . we should see?"

She shook her head again.

"So I guess . . . Should we . . . ?"

We did—out the front doors, back across the cement, and past the silver carts one more time. As hungry as I was, I decided to wait. The desire to drop her off was much stronger than the need for food.

On the ride back, Chrissy looked out the window and I played with the stereo. I had plenty of time to wonder if spending additional time and energy on another member of Michael's family was such good idea. Eventually, we turned down her street and passed her building. I hooked a U-turn and rolled to a stop not too far from the front door.

"You don't need to walk me up," she said, just as I was reaching for my seat belt.

"You're just trying to avoid a goodnight kiss, aren't you?" I said.

Horrible joke. I realize that now, but these things happen when I'm nervous.

Five seconds.

"You can kiss me if you want."

My turn to be caught in the five-second delay—that is, until I saw a hand over her mouth, trying to cover the edges of a smile.

"Hey . . . that's mean!" I said, so relieved I almost did a little dance.

She smiled at her window. I gave her shoulder a little push. And just for a second, as I watched her laugh, kissing her didn't seem so funny anymore. For just a moment, Chrissy was pretty enough to break anybody's heart.

"Remember," she said, still smiling.

She unbuckled her seat belt.

"Remember what?"

"Remember that you're coming to see me again."

"Oh . . . yeah, of course."

Her eyes held me in place—a velvet touch tighter than a hand against my cheek. She smiled and opened her door.

"Next Saturday," she said.

"Next Saturday? Well, actually, I don't know if . . ."

But she was already closing the car door over my excuse.

"Hey . . . wait," I said. "Won't your dad be pissed if I let you walk up alone?"

She leaned back in through the open window. "I'll take care of my dad," she said.

I watched her walk down the sidewalk toward the front door. I made sure she was in before I started to pull out. I could just see her inside the little entryway, pulling her keys out of the second door, then slipping inside and out of sight.

I drifted through town, headed back toward the highway, and twisted around the ramp and into the familiar sludge of traffic. Thinking about it on the way home, I tried to decide whether I had actually agreed to see her next Saturday.

The results were inconclusive.

However, just in case I did end up in Baltimore again, I reluctantly decided to do some planning while I had the time.

Now, what does Chrissy need?

Time away from Dad—that was a given. But what else?

I didn't get very far, though—my mind kept looping back to replay parts of our first "date." Eventually, two images beat out the others. The first: her profile as she poked the tank. The second: her face as she looked back into my car.

"I'll take care of my dad."

I tried to brush them off and wave them away, but they were persistent. I pulled up song after song, trying to block out the images, but I couldn't settle on anything else.

Planning for Michael had been relatively easy. The only real difficulty had been the occasional distraction of an Astronomy lecture.

But Chrissy . . .

I realized her little incident with the fish tank was preventing any real thought. I killed the radio with a poke that would have made Chrissy proud.

What the hell was I whining about, anyway? Even though her "aggressive sightseeing" was a bit of a surprise, as a client, Chrissy was perfect.

Well, maybe not perfect, but she would be far less trouble than Michael.

Michael was far too obstinate. He seemed intent on doing "the right thing" in most situations. I wouldn't have that problem with Chrissy (or if I did, I knew I could get around it pretty quickly). She was much more malleable than Michael—just look at her progress after only one session. Okay, so I'd have to deal with some poking when she got cranky. So what? I could just take her by the pet shop when got mad and let her go to town on the aquariums.

There was nothing to worry about. I had at least a week to plan for our next visit. More if I decided to blow her off.

I *knew* Chrissy would listen to me, unlike Michael. It was obvious that she already had a thing for me, which could be an insurmountable advantage if played correctly. Between her and Dad, it was the perfect summer project—guaranteed not to bore.

Crossing back into Virginia and back on familiar ground, I started to feel more like myself again. I set the possibility of a Saturday visit in the corner, telling myself I'd address it just as soon as I had the time.

Or maybe I'd just slap something together on the ride up.

It didn't really matter, did it?

CHAPTER 16

As it always does, Monday morning came much too quickly. But instead of my usual Monday mood keeping me under the covers until Mom got pissed off, the thought of Michael's forthcoming apology helped me pry myself out of bed. I gave Mom a break, too. I was feeling generous. I even told her in advance that Jack was picking me up (but apparently, not soon enough to avoid a disappointed look).

But strangely, there was no Michael waiting at my locker. In fact, I only saw him once all day, and that was from a distance—not nearly close enough for a pointed rebuff (or rebuke, or whatever).

And although I was really looking forward to swatting his apology attempt right back in his face, I tried to remain positive. No apology on Monday gave me something to look forward to on Tuesday.

But I didn't get one on Tuesday, either. When I arrived, I expected to find him pacing up and down in front of my locker, wringing his hands and putting the finishing touches on his lengthy but heartfelt apology.

No Michael, though—just some owlish kid who looked vaguely familiar in an annoying sort of way standing way too close to my locker.

"Hi," he tried, raising a cautious hand.

"Eat it," I said, borrowing a line from Jack.

Needless to say, I could only be expected to stay positive for so long. And needless to say, it was an unpleasant surprise to find that Mom's papers were starting to contribute to my poor frame of mind.

There was no reason even to think twice about them. For one thing, I seriously doubted Mom would actually go through with something like that. But on the off chance she did manage to show a little backbone, I grudgingly gave the whole thing a few moments of my time. The first thought that surfaced was the possibility of new living arrangements. This was a bit of a bother, since I'm more or less satisfied with my current room. The idea of a downgrade was unappealing to say the least.

And having to deal with Mom or Dad's eventual replacement partners was rather unsavory. But then again, finding ways to torment The Replacements made me smile.

Even so, I was doing my best to avoid Mom, actually using my alarm clock and getting out of the house with the smallest amount of contact possible. By grabbing something on the way out the door and avoiding the breakfast table, I eliminated the possibility of "the conversation" during breakfast.

I could just imagine how she'd break it to me. I'd look up from my burnt toast and notice Mom brushing a tear away. I'd go back to my toast, only to be interrupted by a hoarse request.

"Matthew? Can I talk to you for a moment," she'd say gravely, with just a slight hitch in her voice.

Ignoring my "no," she'd continue.

"Matthew? You know your father and I love you very much. You know that, don't you? But there's something we need to discuss. Something difficult. Something very, very difficult."

God! No one should be subjected to that garbage. It was wretched. It was unconscionable. It was something you'd do to war criminals. Or Michael.

But when nothing like that happened by Wednesday, I let myself relax a little. Dad, as usual, was barely home during the week, and Mom spent most of her time at the kitchen table trying to double the size of her piles.

The subject didn't come up and I didn't ask why. I just put my head down and kept moving.

As for Michael, although we had a close encounter Wednesday— passing each other in the hall, going in opposite directions—I skipped the opportunity to make eye contact. The longer he put it off, the more difficult I was going to make it for him.

I didn't see him at all Thursday.

Friday rolled around, but I was thinking about Saturday. Driving to school in Mom's car, I realized I didn't have any plans yet, either for Chrissy or her father. I decided I'd probably opt out; coming up with an excuse was far less work than drafting a plan on the fly. I hoped Chrissy wouldn't be too upset. Maybe Dad had a fish tank in his room as part of an anger management program.

Walking through the student parking lot, I had a feeling I'd be struck by a mysterious illness Friday evening/Saturday morning and, unfortunately, would be in no condition to travel.

I didn't have time to polish the excuse, however. As soon as I pushed through the doors and into Hamilton, I realized something was off. It was the atmosphere. It just wasn't a typical Friday vibe. In fact, it felt almost exactly like a Monday.

The inside of the school had a gray, rainy feel to it. Almost everyone I passed looked groggy and spent. Usually there were little knots of people everywhere making too much noise and clogging up the halls, but today most of the kids were either by themselves or in twos or threes. And nobody looked very happy.

In Michael's section, the kids seemed even more depressed. I had the same thought every time I passed his way: Did the school purposely herd all the Michaels into one specific location? It's like they were trying to contain a nuclear disaster. *"We've got to find a way to keep them from spreading. We can't have the popular students inhaling their fumes."*

Then, up ahead, I saw a really big knot.

A really big knot of people in the middle of a hall means only one thing: fight.

And somehow, I knew. Even before I started knocking people out of my way, I knew I'd find Michael right in the middle of it.

I have to say, I'm not a big fight fan—school fights are almost always mismatches. Usually, it's some tough guy beating on somebody who doesn't want to be there. Every once in a while, though, two guys who really want to beat the hell out of each other get together, and then it's on.

But I wasn't expecting that kind of fight. The closer I got, the sicker I felt. I may have been through with Michael, but that didn't mean I wanted to see him pounded into the ground.

I pushed through the outer rings and into the final layer. It's weird the way I remember the fight. It's like my mind took still pictures instead of filming the whole thing. The first one probably took the longest to process: Michael standing, someone else on the ground. It looked wrong. My brain kept trying to reverse the two kids, but eventually my eyes insisted and my brain gave up.

I flipped to the next picture. Leonard was on the ground. Michael's arm was cocked and ready. Leonard's were up, trying to soften the impact of the next blow.

On to number three: Leonard lying on the ground, trying to cover his head.

Number Four: Michael's face. His jaw was set and his eyes wide. I didn't like any of the pictures, but this one bothered me more than the others.

And then the pictures went back in time.

I flipped through a stack of them. Leonard pushing Michael into a locker. Leonard hanging out a bus window, shouting at Michael as he walked home. Leonard's face a repulsive mixture of anger and glee. Michael huddled on the ground, Leonard standing over him.

And that brought me back to the moment and the last photo.

Wanda was standing in the first layer of spectators. Like everyone else, she seemed to have trouble accepting what was happening right there on the hallway floor. In my picture, her mouth is slightly open, her eyes wide.

"I wish Michael had let *me* kick his ass," Wanda said afterwards. "That kid would have been way more embarrassed."

But Michael did a pretty good job on his own of humiliating Leonard. Eventually, Leonard stopped moving, but Michael's fists didn't. And even though I hated Leonard, I decided it was time someone stepped in.

I called Michael's name a couple times, but he didn't respond, so I had to get pretty close to the action. Even when Michael heard me and finally tore his eyes from Leonard, it took him a second to come back to earth and recognize what was happening.

"Better clear out," I said, quietly.

He nodded and turned, heading through the ring of people who couldn't get out of his way fast enough.

About thirty seconds after Michael left, my Astronomy teacher, Mrs. Hammerschmidt, showed up.

"What's going on here?" she demanded, her voice shrill.

Then came our P.E. teacher, Mr. Humdinger. (I'm sure if my life depended on it, I could probably remember his name, but let's hope the situation never comes up.) He pulled up beside her, out of breath and definitely not expecting to see Leonard on the floor.

Fortunately, there were plenty of kids who couldn't wait to fill them in. It was definitely a big one: "Local Dork Gives Area Tough Guy the Beating of a Lifetime."

I slipped around the remaining spectators, looking for Michael. Don't ask me why. I just did. I walked down a few hallways, checked the cafeteria, stepped outside, and scanned the student parking lot.

No Michael.

I walked back in, took another tour of the first floor, and gave up. I found myself near an out-of-the-way bathroom and decided I might as well use it. I pushed through the swinging door and reluctantly took a look.

Michael was sitting in a stall, the door opened.

He was just sitting there, staring into space—his pants, by the way, were up, so it wasn't like he was in the middle of something.

"Howdy," I said.

He looked at me but didn't answer.

"Guess I don't have to make up any more stories about what a badass you are, huh?"

One of his hands was swollen as hell. It looked like a big lump of meat on a stick. I leaned against a bathroom sink and waited for him to say something.

When he didn't, I asked, "So what happened out there?"

He sighed and hung his head.

"You'd better tell me now and get your story straight," I said, "because you're going to have to tell it to a bunch of cramped-up administrators in a few minutes. So what the hell happened?"

He gave in. "I don't know," he said. "It was like getting hit from behind. When he said that thing to her . . . The whole thing was like fighting through a wave to get back up."

Wanda filled me in later in the day. Apparently, she'd been talking to Michael when Leonard showed up. As usual, Leonard started to give Michael a bunch of crap, but this time Wanda stuck up for him. They went back and forth a bit, then Leonard tossed a racial bomb, and that's when

Michael went crazy.

"Well, at least you won't have to worry about getting hassled so much anymore," I said.

"I shouldn't have done it," he said.

"What do you mean?"

"I shouldn't have hurt him."

"Michael, I would have done the same thing," I said. "So don't sit here and act like you did something horrible. I just wish you'd done it a long time ago and saved yourself a lot of trouble."

"You can leave if you're going to try and convince me fighting's justified," Michael told the floor.

"Excuse me?"

"You heard me."

"Look at me, Michael."

"No."

"Michael."

"No!" he said. "I'm done listening to you." His eyes flashed. "The experiment's over."

"It wasn't an experiment!" I said.

"Then what was it?"

"I was trying to help you!"

"I didn't need your help!"

We both stopped and listened as our voices ricocheted off the bathroom walls. The place seemed built for sound, which is pretty strange if you think about it. It took our words a while to lose their edge.

"I just felt bad for you, Michael," I said, quietly. I could hear voices outside the door. Our time was almost up.

He nodded. "Thanks."

"I just don't get why fighting back is such a big deal," I said.

"Because it's practicing an eye for an eye and a tooth for a tooth," he said. "Gandhi said that taking an eye for an eye only makes the whole world blind. Jesus said if your enemy slaps your right cheek, offer him your left."

"He wasn't talking about butt cheeks, right?"

Michael looked up, apparently disgusted.

"Okay, sorry. Inappropriate."

He stared for a minute, then said, "You know, this whole time, there's one thing you never really understood. But I don't think I did either until just now."

He made me wait.

"And . . .?" I said.

"I like who I am, and I don't want to change, even if it means getting beat up all the time."

"I wasn't trying to change you—" I started to say, but I was interrupted by Mr. Pawpaw, our overweight, loudmouthed vice principal, charging through the bathroom door. Again, I guess he has another name, but he's also probably the only one who cares.

"You the only one in here?" he sputtered.

"Yep," I said.

"No." Michael's voice came from inside his stall.

I shook my head.

"What was that?" Mr. Pawpaw asked.

I pointed to the stall. Michael peered out.

"Are you Michael Dumb Ass?"

Of course, Dumb Ass isn't Michael's real last name. But it should be.

"Yes," Michael said.

"You need to come with me," Mr. Pawpaw said. "Are you going to have a problem walking down to the office?"

"No."

I could tell he was waiting for something to happen, but Michael just walked over and stood quietly in front of him.

"I want you to stay right in front of me," Pawpaw said, pretending he was a cop.

Michael nodded.

"Okay, let's go. You," he said, pointing at me, "get to class. Now."

"But I have to go poopy," I said.

"Get to class," he said, then disappeared with Michael.

I stood at the sink for a minute. After that, I walked into the stall and sat.

How can he not want to change?

I shook my head.

Michael just couldn't understand that changing your image doesn't mean changing yourself. Image is an act—a smokescreen. If you have to, quote Gandhi and get all out of breath about science-fiction with a trusted adult, but why make your life so hard?

Everyone's got secrets—just do your thing in private. Only when they know what you're really like, do you have problems.

Like I said, I think I might be gay. Does that mean I need to hand out fliers that say, "Hi, I'm Matthew. I might be gay. Please feel free to give me shit about it if you don't like gays"?

But Michael wasn't happy unless everyone knew what books he was currently reading and why, his views on all subjects of social/moral importance, and any other scraps of information he had floating around in his head at the time.

I hopped up from the toilet, deciding it was time to stop hanging out in the school bathroom. Going to class might be helpful. Listening to a teacher drone on and on about something we'd never use again sounded kind of comforting at that point, like a bedtime story.

I passed Michael's locker again on the way. The janitor was already sliding a mop across the hall floor, slowly erasing all traces of the fight. It's weird. All it takes is a mop to remove all physical remnants of something with that much social importance. Just twenty minutes ago, this place was clogged with people. Now it was just me and the janitor.

"You need something?" the janitor asked, looking sideways at me.

"A martini."

"Amen, brother," he said, and went back to mopping.

Class was like I'd hoped—half the kids already hypnotized, the other half talking quietly. I opened a notebook and copied some drawings and symbols I found on the whiteboard. They could have been from yesterday or three days ago, but I figured I needed something in case Mrs. Hammerschmidt started to wander around the classroom.

I copied a chunk from the board, using a pen to mark the spot, then flipped to an unused section near the back of my notebook.

Time to plan—but not for Michael. Time to plan for Chrissy.

But once again, I didn't get very far. The Michael Fight was too fresh, and our conversation in the bathroom too perplexing. I just couldn't help wondering what would happen next.

He'd get suspended—that was a given—but for how long? He'd probably spend most of his suspension time at Flap's bookstore, telling him what a horrible person I was, so that would be fun for both of them.

And Wanda—I had an unpleasant feeling she'd be seeing Michael again. Quite soon, I imagined. In fact, he'd probably have more visitors than he could handle. His mom would probably hover over him. Gut might even show some interest now that Michael had actually stood up for himself. Flap would probably bake a fresh batch of science-fiction books for him every afternoon.

I imagined Flap in an apron. There would, of course, be a message on the front—something like, "Kiss My Flap."

So here I was, stuck in school, while Michael would very shortly be relaxing at home and collecting "concerned visitors" like flies over a fresh carcass.

I scowled. Leaning back, I tossed my pen into the open notebook. Somehow, Michael and his life had found its way into my bloodstream.

Fantastic.

I crossed my arms, closed my eyes, and wondered if there was a cure.

I sighed and waited for the answer to come.

CHAPTER 17

I woke up late on Saturday. I opened my eyes, realized it was Saturday morning, and was happy for about fifteen seconds. I smiled and started to drift back to sleep when Friday hit me like a cold shower. All at once, I remembered Michael, the Fight, and (of all things) Mom's stupid papers.

I flipped over and jerked the covers over my head.

I tried to shove everything into that smelly little bathroom in the back of my head, but there was just too much. Not a chance the door would shut.

I heaved a massive sigh and tossed the covers to one side. I lay still for a while, hoping I might manage to trick my body into falling back asleep if it knew I intended to get up, but no such luck.

I rolled out of bed and trudged into the bathroom. I spent a good half hour in the shower wondering what I was going to do with myself the rest of the day. Stepping out, I still wasn't sure, but I did know I needed to get out of the house.

I was throwing on some clothes when I remembered the Chrissy appointment.

Do I feel like social work today?

I wasn't quite sure. I shrugged and decided to see how I felt in a half hour or so.

I made my way down to the kitchen, hoping to catch either Mom or Dad before the cars disappeared. And yes, I was desperate enough to ask Dad for his car if necessary.

Maybe I'll see if Jack's around, I thought. I wasn't about to hang around the house, but I wasn't sure about going up to Baltimore either.

I slowed a little as I got to the bottom of the stairs. I wasn't in the mood for a Mom encounter, and I was absolutely certain she'd be parked at the kitchen table.

I stopped at the landing and peered in. Then I came out from around the corner and stood in the doorway.

Excellent.

The kitchen was empty and Mom's keys were on the hook.

I almost started to wonder where she was and why she hadn't left an armed guard to look after her piles, but then realized I'd left my phone upstairs in my bedroom. It was ringing when I walked in. Without thinking, I picked it up off the nightstand.

"Matthew's phone—you've reached Matthew's assistant. Who's calling please?" I said crisply, walking around the bed and toward the door.

Pause. "Hello?"

A girl's voice, tentative.

"Yes?"

"Oh . . . I think . . . Is Matthew there?"

It was the pauses that gave it away.

"Chrissy?"

"Hi."

I stopped in the doorway, shoulders slumping dejectedly. I turned back and shuffled back into my room, toward the window. *Why the hell did I pick it up? I always look at the number first.*

"Hey, what's going on?" I asked, slipping into my best sick voice.

And how did she get my number, anyway?

"Not much," she said. Then, a few beats later, "I guess."

"You guess? You're not sure?" I asked, smiling a little.

At the window, I lifted the end of a slat. Peering out through the opening in the blind, I began to reconsider. It might be possible to muster up the energy for a trip to Baltimore; at least it would get me out of the house.

"No," she said.

"Okay," I said, laughing a little. "Any reason you're not sure?"

Talking to Chrissy was so different than talking to Wanda or Jack. What with the pauses and processing, it was like listening to an interview on satellite phone. I wasn't used to the pace or the down time between our sentences. It was like playing a team so far below your skill level they keep tripping you up.

"I wanted to talk about today," she said.

"Yeah, sure," I said, keeping a trace of illness in my voice in case I needed an out.

"I don't . . ." she began.

I waited.

"I don't think we should see each other this weekend," she said.

I dropped the slat I'd been holding.

"Why?" I asked, one eyebrow up. "Got some other plans?" I walked to the other side of the room. "Ditching me for some other guy, maybe?"

"Matthew . . ."

"Kidding," I said, adding a fake laugh just to illustrate what a kidder I am. But it sounded atrocious. *What the hell?*

I sat down on my bed and started fiddling with the alarm clock on my nightstand.

"Still there?" I asked, smiling. But it was all teeth.

"Yes," she said, her voice soft.

"Oh. Got something going on with Dad," I said, nodding.

"No."

I stopped nodding.

"So what's up?" I asked.

I should have sounded breezy, but I didn't. I stopped playing with the clock and straightened some pillows.

I waited, but not long enough. Just as I finally said "Hello?," she said, "Michael called last night."

I stood.

That explains the phone number.

"Did he now?" I asked, wandering into my bathroom.

"Yes."

"What for? To talk to your dad?"

"Yes."

"Oh. Okay. How'd that go?" I said, stopping in front of my sink. I glanced at myself in the mirror, but quickly turned away. I hopped up onto the counter instead, feet dangling.

I waited.

"It was fine," she said, then added, "He talked to me, too."

"Ahh," I said, quietly. *Now I get it.* "What did you guys talk about?" I asked.

And before she could answer:

"Did he need some information? I think he's doing a paper on sea-horses."

Pause.

"What?"

"Nothing," I said, closing my eyes. "So, what did he want?" I said, loud and slow.

"He wanted to talk about you."

My turn to pause.

I hopped down off the counter.

"Bet that was fun," I said.

"No. Not really."

"You sure about that?" I asked.

Pause.

"Why would it be fun?" she asked, and then added, "What's that noise?'

"What noise?"

"That one."

"What . . . my mouth?" I said.

"No, that tapping."

"'Tapping'?"

I was in front of the mirror again. There was a toothbrush in my hand. Apparently, I'd been hammering it on the counter.

"I don't know," I lied, tossing the toothbrush into the sink. "Could be the front door. Michael comes over on the weekend for our counseling sessions."

"Matthew?"

"You know me," I said, voice rising. "Always trying to better myself."

I came out of the bathroom and over to my dresser.

I should probably skip Baltimore, I thought, opening drawers. *Maybe see what Jack's up to. Or Wanda.*

Pause.

"Still there?" I asked.

"Yes."

"So you talked about me, huh? Sounds fun," I said.

"Matthew, please stop saying that . . . We didn't talk *about* you," she said.

"You lost me," I said. Then, "Hey, now I know how it feels to be—" I stopped myself, but I couldn't tell whether she caught it or not.

"We . . ." she began. "He just wanted to tell what happened."

"Ah, yes. What happened," I said, sagely, shoving a drawer back into place, then pulling out another. "What happened when? At lunch? During our sessions? I hope not, because he promised our sessions were confidential. He signed a paper, you know."

I looked down into the open drawer. *What am I looking for anyway?*

"No, you don't understand—"

"It's okay, Chrissy. I get it," I said. "Michael called to 'warn' you, right? He called to tell you what a shithead I am and a grifter and that I'm a dangerous influence and how you shouldn't—"

"That's *not* what happened!"

Oops. She's angry. Maybe even aquarium angry.

I plopped down on the foot of my bed, a hand on my forehead.

What the hell? How did I let this get away from me?

The answer was right there, of course.

Michael.

"Sorry," I said, pulling my shit together.

I put the ass-kicking Michael had earned to one side and shook my head. *Get into the game, for Christ's sake!*

"No," she said, "I'm sorry. I can't say what I—"

"Don't apologize," I said, gently, *thinking how great it would be to call Michael this afternoon when Chrissy and I were sitting on her couch in Baltimore, enjoying a beer and a music lecture from Dad.*

I just needed a new approach.

"It's my fault," I admitted. "Guess I was just upset. I think I was just looking forward to our da—to today," I said sweetly. "And got pissed when you canceled. Sorry. I know I'm a jackass."

"Matthew . . ." she said, but I could tell she was smiling.

"There you go," I said. "That's better." Then, just a little softer: "Remember the first time I saw you."

Pause.

"Yes."

"Remember what happened?"

I waited.

Eventually, she laughed.

"Are you laughing at me, young lady?" I said.

"No!"

"Because as I remember it, you got to go to your room. I had to stand in the hall."

She was really laughing now.

"That's better," I said, lying back on the bed. "I'll have to remember that."

Wait for her . . .

"Remember what?" she asked.

"Remember to say 'jackass' whenever you're angry at me."

She laughed again. I awarded myself a point.

Okay, easy now . . .

"You say it," I said.

"No!"

"Come on. Don't be shy. It's fun. *Matthew's a jackass.*"

I waited. "Well?"

"No," she said, her voice flat.

And just like that, we were where we'd started.

Damn it, I thought, standing. *Too much. Idiot.*

I had to stop making so many mistakes.

"Matthew, you have to let me explain," she said, for about the fiftieth time.

"Of course," I said.

"Michael just wanted—he wasn't trying to be mean or anything—he just wanted to tell me about . . . about what happened."

"I get it. Seriously, I do."

"Really?"

"Absolutely. Michael just wanted to fill you in. Kind of let you know what's been happening with him, right—him and me," I added, graciously.

"Yes," she said, sounding relieved.

A half-point for me.

"And you just want some time to think. About what Michael said."

"Yes."

"So you want to reschedule our da—I mean, put off our . . . visit."

"Yes . . . well, I don't know if we . . ."

"No, you're right," I said.

I was by the window again.

What's it like outside? I wonder if I should wear shorts?

"Listen," I said, "if Michael thinks we should put it off until next weekend, then I think we should."

Pause.

"Well, that's not—"

"No. I think he's right," I said.

Pause.

"Michael didn't tell me to do that," she said.

I smiled.

"Oh, he . . . Sorry, I thought he wanted you to . . .?"

"He just told me—"

"What happened. Right. I get it. Makes sense," I said, wandering past the dresser to the other side of the room.

"Do you? Really?"

"Of course," I said. "Absolutely. You talked to Michael, he decided I was a terrible person, and—"

"No!"

"Oh . . . sorry," I said, adding just the right amount of confusion. "But I thought . . ."

"I do like you, Matthew."

"You do?"

"Yes. I do."

"Thanks."

I waited a moment. Then: "Because that's what—I mean, I thought you and Michael had decided . . .?"

"No," she said firmly. "I decided. I'm the one who decided we shouldn't see each other today."

I jammed a hand into the side of the dresser as I walked by.

Damn it!

"That's why I don't want to see you today," she explained.

Okay, I said, forcing myself to breathe. *Not a problem. I just need a different angle.*

"I just need some time," she said.

"Uh-huh."

"To think about things."

"Sure."

Okay, where's that different angle? I had her a minute ago. Why isn't anything coming?

"Thanks, Matthew."

"Yeah, sure. But wait a minute—don't I get a chance to give you my side?" I said.

Pause.

"No."

"No?" I laughed.

"I'll listen to you. I promise. Just not yet."

Pause.

"Will you not be mad?" she asked. "Will you give me time?"

I opened my mouth, but nothing useful came out.

"Guess I'll have to," I managed.

"Thanks, Matthew."

"Oh, sure. My pleasure."

"Don't be mad," she said again.

"I'll do my best," I said, sourly.

"Please don't."

Think of something!

But nothing came.

"Okay."

"I'll call you?" she said.

"Yeah, sure. When?"

Pause.

"I don't know . . . I'm sorry."

"Oh, it's okay. It's Michael's fault anyway, right?"

That one fell flat on its face.

"I'll call you," she promised.

And then she hung up.

I was by the window. I reached for the vertical plastic rod and started twisting it, opening and shutting the blinds.

"Ridiculous," I said, twisting it one way, then the other. Turning it to the limit, then turning it a little more.

I let it fall back against the slats and tugged on the cord. Lifting the blinds a few inches, then releasing them. I'm not sure how long I stood there, but after a while, I wandered back to my bed.

I sat on the edge, staring at the blank TV screen. I laid the phone to one side and picked up the remote.

Actually, I'm glad she canceled, I thought. *Saved me the trouble, and I still have the sick card for another occasion.*

No, really. This is good.

No more trips to Baltimore. No more uncomfortable phone calls, drunken dads, or aquarium security guards.

For a while, I mean. Just a little break.

No more Michael, no more half-sisters, no more members of the Michael Clan. Now I can spend time on me instead.

I sat at the foot of my bed and started watching another *Pawn Stars*, but was back at the blinds after only a few minutes.

Twisting the rod.

Thinking.

Michael.

I heard a *pop*. I dropped the rod and let it swing back against the blind. It dangled awkwardly.

"Ridiculous," I said.

CHAPTER 18

I hope you're not expecting a moral to this story. Because I'm the one telling it, not Michael.

If he was telling it, I'm sure he'd include a moral. Probably something like, "Be happy with yourself and tell everyone about it. Or, "Appreciate people for who they are instead of trying to change them."

So if you're the type of person who needs a moral, how's this? I tried to help Michael. It worked for a while, and then he messed things up. The moral? "Be very selective if you're thinking of helping anyone."

Of course, if this was a movie, I would have pulled Michael from a burning building by now (or vice versa), and we'd have put aside our differences, embraced, and become friends for life.

But it isn't a movie.

I knew Michael would get suspended. That was a given. Leonard, too.

However, I had a bad feeling Michael's life would probably be a lot better from here on out.

I mean, I was pretty sure people wouldn't be picking on him for a while. The rumor (*my* rumor, in fact) had already made that so, but after what happened with Leonard, I doubted anyone wanted to risk a beat down from Michael. They'd completely lose their place in the food chain.

So that was something.

Oh, and Wanda.

Thanks to me, Michael knew Wanda. Not only did he know her, apparently she could actually stomach being around him for more than two minutes.

(Which reminded me, I really needed to speak to her about that.)

And his dad, right? He knew his dad now.

And Chrissy . . .

So all that time and attention, and all that success, and Michael *still* had the balls to kick me to the curb.

Well, anyway, Monday showed up way too soon. The only thing that made it manageable was vacation from Michael.

That, and I figured I'd probably get a call from Chrissy in a couple of days. There was still plenty of time to win that one. Unlike her ingrate of a half-brother, I knew Chrissy would apologize. And even though I wouldn't answer the initial call, I decided to be lenient with her. She'd leave a message. I'd be nice and call her back in a day or two.

Wednesday came. Even though it was still a little early, a call wouldn't have taken me completely by surprise. So I didn't think much of it when she didn't.

Thursday, I told myself as I was falling asleep. *Definitely Thursday.*

But no call Thursday either. Near the end of the day, I checked my phone for messages, figuring one might have slipped past me.

No message.

By Friday afternoon, I *still* hadn't heard anything and was starting to simmer.

Once again, Michael had managed to irritate me, this time remotely. I was sure I'd get a call Friday night, but on the off chance I didn't, I decided to take Mom's car Saturday morning and make one last visit to Michael's crappy house.

I didn't bother thinking up a plan to get past Gut or persuade Michael to let me in. I'd break that fucking door down, tap dance on Gut, and drag Michael kicking and screaming from under his bed.

For all I knew, Michael had called Chrissy again just to make she understood the "danger" of getting involved with someone like me. By 9:00 Friday night, I was sure he had. A week had gone by and the only explanation that made any sense was Michael butting in yet again.

I was past simmer now. I'd reached a rolling boil, and the only thing that kept me from roaring over to Michael's Friday night was the fact that Mom had actually gone out with some of her friends for the evening. Dad was, of course, elsewhere. Well, that and the fact that Michael was probably already in bed snoring peacefully.

I'll give her until noon Saturday. Just to be sure.

(I was pretty mad, but not mad enough to get up early on a weekend.)

But I was up early Saturday.

If it's the weekend and I'm alert and awake before 8:30, I know it's going to be a bad day.

Refusing to be pushed around by whatever body part was unable to be quiet and let me sleep, I flipped over and tried to get comfortable. I stayed still for a while and glared at the ceiling. When that didn't work, I tried almost every sleeping position known to man.

But instead of finding the right one, all the movement just added to my insomnia. I made one last angry flip and vowed to stay put until either sleep returned or my bladder burst. But my last flip brought me face to face with my window.

And as I studied the light that had somehow managed to sneak through the blinds, my eyes settled on the broken twisty rod. And that stupid twisty rod shoved me right back into Chrissy's absurd phone call.

Michael and his nonsense had me up and in a shitty mood before 9:00 on a Saturday.

I jerked out of bed and started pulling on clothes.

Time for one last visit.

I cleaned myself up as best as I could, though I didn't have much patience for it. I grabbed my music and was quickly out of my room, down the stairs, and into the kitchen. I was so caught up with Michael that I forgot to peer in first.

"Wow, you're up early," Mom said. One of her many tired old jokes.

As usual, she was at the table.

"Back already?" I asked. "How was girls' night out? Hit any strip clubs?"

I grabbed her keys from off the hook and turned to go.

"Are you taking the . . . Matthew! Get back here!"

I stopped and backed into the kitchen. I don't know why I didn't just bolt for the door. I wasn't thinking straight. Heaving a massive sigh, I turned to face her.

"So, I guess you're going out," she said.

"Nope, just taking the keys for a little walk."

"Where are you going?"

"To see a dear friend."

I turned.

"Matthew!"

"Yes?"

"Who?"

"Michael."

"Who's Michael?"

"New kid at school. You'd love him."

"Really? When am I going to meet him?"

"Maybe we'll visit him at the hospital," I said.

"What?"

"Nothing. Can I go now?"

"No. When are you coming back?"

"I don't know. A couple hours?"

"How about lunchtime?" she said.

"Yeah, sure," I said.

Just get out of my way or, so help me, I'm going to run you over.

"Matthew! I'm going to take those keys if you keep turning your back on me."

"Yes, Mother," I said. "What is it now?"

"I want you back at lunch, okay? Really."

"God! I told you I'd be back. What else do you want?"

Watching her cringe, like I was an unstable dog that had just tried for her nose, almost pushed me over the edge. Keeping my voice in check took every ounce of self-control I had left.

"What?" I managed, pushing the words through my teeth.

She opted for a dramatic pause, before saying, "It's important," in a meek little voice.

I endured her Look of Concern as long as I could.

"Why? What's going on?" I demanded.

"There's a reason I want you back by lunch. I want to make sure we have a chance to talk today."

I didn't say anything right away. I should have said, "Okay, fine," but instead I said, "Why?"

"There's something we need to discuss," she said, eyes dropping down to her piles.

"What?" I asked.

"Just something we need to discuss," she repeated. "I don't want to talk about it now, okay?"

"No," I said. "Not okay! I don't have time for this crap!"

The hurt on her face just made me angrier. "Matthew . . . why are you—"

"Just shut up and leave me the hell alone."

I turned and stalked down what little hall there was, threw the garage door open, and slammed the hell out of it after I was through.

I hopped into the car, clicked the button for the garage door, and pulled out before it was all the way up. Out on the street, as I was jerking the car into drive, I detected movement in the garage.

Glancing over as I pulled away, I saw Mom standing in the pocket door, eyes wide, mouth partially open. I didn't bother to award myself any points. I didn't feel like playing the Game today.

We're so close to the Beltway that it's almost always the first leg of any trip. I'd driven this stretch so many times that I was fairly certain I could pull out of our neighborhood and onto the exit ramp with my eyes closed. Today, I was almost pissed enough to finally try, but I wasn't about to do anything that might delay my little visit with Michael.

Merging into the line of traffic, I loaded my music and went right to the Album—the one I only play three times a year.

The Unforgettable Fire. Not the whole album, mind you, just a chunk. Songs four through seven.

I guess some people have a favorite song. I have four and they just happen to be right next to each other.

I never want to get tired of these songs, so I only let myself listen to them three times a year. But it was late spring and I'd already listened to them twice—not a good sign.

Barring any pile-ups or road work, the trip would be a quick one. It was only one exit away—the exit that would take me past school and, eventually, to Michael's.

I stomped on the accelerator. The exit came up fast. I hauled the car into the right-hand lane and started to slow.

Then I took my foot off the brake and let my car slide right past the exit.

I guess maybe I needed a little time—time to think, time to draw up a basic plan. As I mentioned, I'm not big on improv.

There was another exit less than a mile away. I decided to take that one instead and make my way back toward school without the assistance of the Beltway. It would give me just enough time to plan.

I stayed in the right lane, ready to exit. I even hit the turn signal. But I didn't take this ramp off the Beltway either. I just kept going.

I lost a bunch of anger after that. I wasn't sure what I was doing, but figured I'd find out soon enough. So I just drove, soaking up the Album, head empty.

It was a nice feeling that didn't last very long. Once I crossed the bridge that separated Virginia from Maryland, I suddenly realized where I was headed.

As soon as I crossed the border, I reached for the radio. I stopped the Album, took it back to the first song, and let it go.

And for some reason, when I think back on that day, deciding to play the Album in its entirety always stands out as one of the strangest things.

By the time the Album was done, I was pretty close.

I took a quick look inside my head, wondering if I had a plan.

Nope.

No plan, but there *was* something. A little speck hidden under something old and dusty. Something from a long time ago, but something immediately familiar. And when I blew the dust off and looked at it for the first time in years, I almost threw it into the darkest corner I could find.

But I didn't.

Instead, I held it in one hand. It bulged, then pulsed into an idea.

No, I thought immediately, *this is ridiculous. It's stupid. No way.*

But now that I'd uncovered it, the idea seemed to have a life of its own. It began to grow, pushing outward in quick jerks. And by the time I found her exit, I had given in.

At the bottom of her ramp, I looked for a place to pull over.

I found a 7-Eleven, or something that used to be a 7-Eleven before someone pulled the logo down. They hadn't bothered to paint over the outlines, however, and I wondered if they really thought the general public would believe it was an independent convenience store that just happened to have the same attractive green and orange color scheme.

I had my phone out almost before the car stopped rolling.

I tried to remember the name of Michael's bookstore but quickly gave up. Baltimore was a pretty big city. There were other stores. And as long as they had what I needed, it didn't matter which one I chose.

It didn't take long. I pulled a scrap of paper out of the glove compartment and jotted down a few names and numbers I pulled up on my phone.

I found one on the second try.

Yes, they carried them. Yes, they were pretty close. I didn't ask if they had the guy I was looking for. It didn't really matter. As long as they carried them, I could make it work.

I wasn't about to drive back home and get mine.

I told them where I was and scribbled a few basic directions. I managed to find the place without too much trouble. Finding a parking spot was another matter. It was on a one-way street; there were parallel lines of parked cars on either side next to a string of parking meters. Several blocks of specialty stores were packed as tightly as the cars flanking them.

Somehow, I managed to squeeze into something that was probably a space. After that, I was in and out of the store in under ten minutes.

Not only did they have plenty, but they had the guy I was looking for.

Back in the car, I retraced my steps back to Sort of 7-Eleven. My hand went to the radio again and the Album came to life.

This time, just four through seven.

I floated quietly toward her apartment. Back down streets that were becoming familiar, past a few landmarks. At some point, I crossed the line but wasn't paying attention. Down her street and past her apartment. One U-turn later and I was rolling by her building, taking the first right and gently coming to a stop on the usual side street.

I sat in the car a while, looking at the glass vestibule, then down at the little bag on the passenger seat.

I opened the glove compartment and rummaged around until I

found something I could use. Thankfully, it was a grocery store receipt, so there was plenty of space on the back.

I thought for a while, but it didn't take long. On the back of the receipt, I wrote:

Chrissy,

This is for you. He was my favorite when I was a ~~little~~ younger. Guess I still like him. Hope you do, too. Just don't tell anyone, okay (ha,ha)? Actually, tell anyone you want. I don't care anymore.

Matthew

I took the comic book out of the bag and tucked the note inside the front cover. I left the top of it sticking out—just enough so her name was out. Then I hopped out of the car.

Inside the vestibule, I reached for the buzzer but couldn't push it.

What the hell are you doing? Will you look at yourself, for Christ's sake? Standing there with a comic book in one hand, suddenly feeling like the biggest idiot in the world.

Get back in the car before it's too late!

I brought the comic book a little closer to my face.

The Silver Surfer.

I opened the door just a crack to my smelly little bathroom. Just enough room for a few memories to slip out.

Sitting on the floor of my bedroom, staring at the panels and thinking the Silver Surfer was the coolest guy in the world. Wondering what it would feel like to surf through the universe. Wondering what his planet Zenn-La was like. Desperately wishing I could leave this world and visit.

I thought I could handle the memories, but they were too potent. And they felt so *ridiculous*, I dropped the book on the floor of the vestibule and turned to go. I was almost out when I heard the security door pop open behind me.

An older woman, black curls, enormous purse slung over one shoulder.

I turned and caught the edge of the door before it was too late.

Holding on with one hand, I scooped up the comic book before she could step on it and jumped inside.

"Hey," the woman barked, "what are you doing? Do you live here?"

Fortunately, she wasn't concerned enough to chase me up the stairs.

Finding Chrissy's floor, stifling the voice inside my head, the one demanding that I cease and desist.

At her door and breathing hard, I knelt and slipped the comic book underneath, sliding the top half into her apartment. I slapped a hand over the voice in my head and held on until I was at the bottom of the stairs pushing through the vestibule. Then I let it go.

But nothing came. It had nothing to say anymore.

Out the door and back into the car. I figured the voice was just catching its breath. I was sure it would kick up as soon as I started the car, yelling that it was my last chance, demanding I rush back up and get the comic book before it was too late.

But it didn't.

Actually, my head felt incredibly light the entire ride home. I peeked in the smelly little bathroom, but for the moment, it was empty. I had the Album on again. I was way over my limit, but I didn't care.

About five minutes after I got home, the phone rang.

I picked it up on the second ring.

acKnowLedgments

This book is humbly dedicated to the following:

To Bruce, who restored my faith in many things.

To Harrison, without whom this book would not exist.

To Chris, who pulled it from the slush pile.

To my father, for reading me *The Hobbit*.

To my mother, for passing on a love of books.

To my sister, for her lifelong support.

To Brian W., who was and still is one of my best friends.

To Joe K., a loyal friend who came through when no one else would.

For all the members of the All Night Crew . . . "You can't leave yet! Dave's not even on!"

To Shane, for keeping me alive.

To Susan, who knows why.

To John W., one of the most important people in my life.

To Robert H., one of the greatest storytellers on the planet.

To Kate, who helped me realize many dreams.

And to Jeff K., whose continuing influence pervades and whom I miss more every year.

About the Author

Jeff Schilling was born in San Diego, California, but grew up in Falls Church, Virginia. He remembers lying in bed, listening to his father read *The Hobbit* to him, and can still recall how it felt to hear that story for the first time. And though he always wished he was someone who knew exactly what he wanted to do from a very early age, he wasn't. But he did love music, reading, and football.

He was quiet and unremarkable during his middle and high school years. After graduation, he attended Virginia Tech and chose English as his major because he still liked to read and nothing else seemed terribly appealing. While attending Virginia Tech, he managed to take one Creative Writing course, but was secretly put out when his professor didn't find his work to be astonishing.

After college, he worked as a waiter, dialysis clerk, purchasing assistant, case manager, and in a number of cubes before deciding he'd better find something he liked. He still loved books and music, but decided to write since he didn't play an instrument, is terrified of doing anything in front of an audience, and isn't good at staying up late. Unfortunately, he wasn't able to quit his day job to pursue this endeavor, because no one was willing (or able) to support him. He did, however, manage to break free of the cubicle and has worked with children for the past ten years, writing when he can.

Jeff claims that, if he'd known it would take this much work and so many years to achieve his goal, he might have given up long ago. After many manuscripts, two halfway decent, self-published books, and hundreds of rejection letters, he was fortunate enough to come to the attention of Bruce Bortz, publisher of Bancroft Press, and his tremendously gifted editor, Harrison Demchick. The patience and perseverance the author cultivated during the edit and rewrite process for *Changing Michael*, the author believes, were probably good for him.

Jeff is currently living in Denver, Colorado with his wife, daughter, house rabbit, and two guinea pigs. His day job is teacher's assistant and teacher of creative writing. He hopes to write a few more books . . . if anyone's interested. He also hopes that this vague and unremarkable biography might inspire other closeted artists. If it could happen to him, it could happen to anybody. *Really.*